PRETTY New DOLL

Be my pretty new doll — Ker Dukey

KER DUKEY & K WEBSTER

Pretty New Doll
Copyright © 2017 Ker Dukey and K. Webster

Cover Design: All By Design
Photo: Adobe Stock
Editor: Word Nerd Editing, www.wordnerdediting.com
Formatting: Champagne Formats

ISBN-13:978-1548781361
ISBN-10:1548781363

ALL RIGHTS RESERVED. This book contains material protected under International and Federal Copyright Laws and Treaties. Any unauthorized reprint or use of this material is prohibited. No part of this book may be reproduced or transmitted in any form or by any means, electronic or mechanical, including photocopying, recording, or by an information and retrieval system without express written permission from the Author/Publisher.

This is a work of fiction. Names, characters, places, and incidents either are the product of the author's imagination or are used fictitiously, and any resemblance to actual persons, living or dead, business establishments, events, or locales is entirely coincidental.

Warning:

To fully enjoy this title, you need to have read *Pretty Stolen Dolls* followed by *Pretty Lost Dolls,* and be fucked up enough to want more.

This book has some disturbing scenes that can cause triggers to the sensitive reader, but if you read and survived the first two books with no psychotic breaks, you'll be just fine…*maybe.*

Please read with caution and we ask that you keep any reviews spoiler free so others can experience the story as it happens. Remember, those who spoil call the wrath of Benny upon themselves…

Thank you so much for reading and supporting our thrilling series!

DEADICATION

For all the little dollies who are sick, sick, sick,
Who demanded more Benny to come quick, quick, quick,
K&K took the hint and began to plot, plot, plot,
And along came the story smoking hot, hot, hot.
Putting fingers to keyboard, they would type, type, type,
With hopes their story lives up to the hype, hype, hype.
So run little dolly to your bed, bed, bed,
And don't come out until the story is read, read, read.

"I do know the difference between right and wrong, but I just like the way wrong feels. It's an impulse, an urge more intense than anything else."
~Benny
(*Pretty Lost Dolls* by Ker Dukey and K Webster)

PROLOGUE

~ New ~

Benny

THE TIGHTNESS OF THE SKIN on my right shoulder pulls, restricting my movements. The phantom pain humming in awareness of past wounds simmers as I bend to snap a blade of grass from the position I've been in for the previous four hours.

Situated yards from my old home—*our* old home—I linger, waiting, knowing, wanting.

Popping the lid from a bottle of water, I gulp down the liquid and pour the remaining dregs over my head, relishing in the reprieve from the heat.

The sun is unforgiving, summoning memories of the first day I ever saw my dirty little doll. She was so young, fresh-faced, perfect.

Pretty little doll.

When the sun would catch the wet strands laced with sweat just right, her hair looked like it had glimmers of gold throughout it. The summer dress she wore clung to her petite structure like a second skin, outlining her perfect little frame.

And then there was her younger sister…

Broken dolly.

She was stroking her small hands over my works of art, her gasp echoing in the thick air as her arms encircled one of my favorite dolls, clinging to the porcelain perfection.

"Pretty doll for a pretty doll," I offered in a soft tone.

In unison, their eyes lifted to gaze at me, and my heart thundered in my chest.

Thud.

Thud.

Thud.

The doll was now forgotten as they both studied me grinning down at them.

"She can't afford the doll," my perfect little doll barked, narrowing her gaze, but the flush of her cheeks gave her away. She knew right then whom she belonged to, and I knew she was mine.

How easy it was to take what I wanted, and how easily she ruined us years later.

She's changed so much since then. The years passed too quickly. I didn't get enough time with her.

The memory fades as a flock of birds take flight from a tree behind the ruins of the house where I wait with the patience I've let build over the years. I've come so far since the night she killed me.

She didn't even clean up the aftermath of her treachery. They didn't even come looking for my remains.

She just left me to die and thought that would be it.

She was so fucking wrong. They both were.

Amateurs.

Three Years Ago

"What are you doing?" I ask, my brow dipping as I study her. She looks defiant, something clear and almost peaceful in her eyes. She locked us inside.

"I'm making us face what we've done," she hisses. "We are locked in here to atone."

Fucking atone? She doesn't understand. I had to kill Macy. She was broken—too unstable to risk being around her.

I loved her too in my own way. Why doesn't she understand?

Squeezing my eyes closed, my fists smash against my face to stop the screaming inside my brain.

"But she was broken. We couldn't fix her," I tell her through clenched teeth.

She growls back at me. "You're the fucking broken one, Benny. You. Are. Broken."

My bones harden, and the blood coagulates inside my veins like cement. "Don't you dare say that."

A sob rips through her as her legs wobble. "We have your dad," she spits out through a rainstorm of tears. "He's been raping girls for years, and you just let that pervert live. After everything he did to Bethany," she cries, pointing an accusing finger at me. My eyes hone in on the judgmental digit. It may as well be a knife the way she wields it with the power of its sharp edge.

Bethany was sacred, and she's using her to hurt me because she's hurting, but she will learn she doesn't need

Macy. She has me, and we're all we need. Together, we will be forever.

My father had his uses, but we didn't need him either. I'd kill him for her, if that's what it took for her to come home, but it's all too late. The tide has changed; its undercurrent is too forceful to manipulate.

"He was useful," I tell her.

"You disgust me," she bites back, *but it's just the brief anger. It will pass.*

"Well, that will change," I placate, taking a step toward her.

"No," she snaps, holding her hand up to stop my advance—the hand free of the cuffs once decorating her wrists.

"It ends tonight, dirty little doll," I warn her.

"You're right." She jerks her head and lets out a harsh laugh. "It does."

Bending down, I retrieve the syringe from my sock.

"What the hell is that?" she demands, gesturing for it as I right myself.

My eyes narrow on the gun she's holding, then to the space behind the bars.

The kid is gone.

She's not alone.

How could she fucking betray me?

"You didn't come alone?" I ask in disbelief. *She's breaking the rules—she knows what happens when she breaks the rules.*

"I'll never be alone again," she jeers. "Dillon is part of me. He's who I belong with. It was never you, Benjamin."

Argh! How dare she say his name to me.

She belongs to me. She is my doll. My dolly!

My jaw clenches as fury rages through every muscle coiling in my body. "I'll never let you leave this cell," *I promise on a warning.* "Never."

Her hand moves, wiggling the gun in her hand. "I'm the one holding the gun. You have no power over me anymore."

A smirk tugs at my lip. "Even if you get a round off, I'll still advance and stick this in you. We're going out together. Eternity will be enough time for you to realize it's me you love."

Her eyes twitch as she weighs up her options.

You don't have any! We belong together and you know it!

I move to advance on her, but she blurts out words that send me spinning. "I'm pregnant."

My arm drops as her confession saturates me in new possibilities. A pop rings out sharp in my ear as burning fire penetrates my shoulder, pulling me backwards.

Fuck.

"Goddammit!" *I snarl.* "You fucking shot me!" *The needle clatters to the floor as I stumble back and fall onto the bed without control.*

"Damn right," *she says with pride as she strides toward me, stopping to stamp her boot on the syringe.*

She has my baby inside her—our baby.

"You're pregnant? We made a baby...?"

A cold snap of a cuff closes around my wrist, and I just watch her, mystified by her news.

She cuffs my other hand, the faint humming of pain throbbing in my shoulder as she pushes my body to the floor.

We're going to have a baby.

The door behind her clicks open, and the stinking pig

Dillon moves in behind her. How dare he interrupt this moment for us?

I'm going to kill him slow, make him feel my wrath with every cut of my knife.

He won't take this moment away from us.

"Our baby," I murmur, staring up at my beautiful doll.

Dillon steps around her, blocking her from view as he collects the broken dead doll from the bed, then walks out of the room, leaving only the two of us, like it's supposed to be.

"The baby isn't yours, Benny," she spits out. "Death can't exist within life. And no matter how many different ways you try to snuff out my existence with your monstrosities, you'll never succeed. You belong in hell. Your time here on earth is over. This baby is life. This baby is no part of you."

My mouth opens, but pain too strong cripples my insides, robbing me of my voice. She's lying. She can't mean that.

She's moving out of the room, backing away while aiming her gun at me. She doesn't need the gun; she's already killing me with her words. Once the door is shut and locked into place, Dillon reappears, placing his disgusting lips to her head.

"It's okay," she tells him. "I've got this."

"I know you do," he murmurs before stalking off to leave her with who she truly belongs to.

She knows who her master is and that our baby grows inside her womb.

"You're lying," I inform her. My strength returning, I pull at the stupid cuffs she thinks can hold me.

Silly little doll.

Struggling to get to my feet, the annoying pain radiating out from the hole she put in me, I force my body to move while she glares down at me.

She's playing games, and I don't like it.

"Let me fucking go," I growl out my command. "Now!"

The laugh that escapes her reminds me of her sister. It's crazed, like she's losing her hold on reality. He's broken her. Changed her. But she will come to her senses. I know it.

"You have no power. I'm going to leave you to rot here. Just like you did us. I hope the stench of my baby sister's blood haunts you until you die of starvation."

She wouldn't dare.

I tug again at the cuffs.

"Let me fucking go." I charge the door, throwing my body against it. It doesn't move, but I knew it wouldn't. These doors are impenetrable. I built them to keep my dolls safely inside.

"I said let me go!" I warn once more.

"You never let me go…" her voice cracks. "Goodbye, Benny."

And then, she abandons me, but she knows I'll come for her. That's why she hasn't killed me. Despite her ramblings—the poison Detective Piece of Shit has fed her into thinking otherwise—she loves me and wants me to come for her.

"Come back, dirty doll! Open the door!" I shout, while snapping my thumb out of place and forcing the cuff from my hand. It tears at the flesh, leaving a blood trail down my hand, the stinging discomfort only fueling my rage.

The thing about this room is it belonged to her sister—not her.

My broken dolly only got punished with confinement when she was a bad dolly. Other than that, she was free to roam. Her key was only taken if she was being punished.

Searching the small space, it takes no time at all to locate the small doll with its eye missing and scissors sticking through the middle.

Around its neck on a small chain is the room key.

Even in death, my broken doll was loyal and serving to her master.

Getting to the door, I unlock the latch and stop moving. Ash and burning wood assaults my nostrils, the scent intense and sticking to the back of my throat. Heat builds under my foot as orange flames ignite, bordering the entire house.

I'm surrounded by fire, destroying everything I built.

How could she do this? This was her home too.

She thinks I'm locked in here.

She wants to kill me.

No. She can't. She wouldn't.

The burning wrath engulfs the house, licking at my skin as I battle through the raging inferno to the beckoning protection of the cold air outside.

Glass shatters as the whining of the tortured wood screams and whimpers all around me.

The smoke, thick and deadly, cloaks me as I run toward a window and crash through it.

The shards tear and rip at the damaged flesh of my arms, but I'm almost numb to the pain. To the heartache. Numb to my dirty little doll.

I lay there, on the grass, staring up at the sky as billowing black smoke turns day to night, just a couple meters from the devastation and remnants of the only home I've ever known.

She killed me.

My pretty little doll killed me.

Shaking my head to clear the memory, I scan the destroyed area.

This is my gravesite. My haunting ground that she visits. No matter what she tells herself, or what he tells her, she is and will always be mine, and my signature on her soul calls her here.

She will come here. I know it.

She returned last year, and I watched—watched tears bubble and fall, accompanied by an unnatural sob that changed to a laugh. She shook her head and tucked a strand of hair behind her ear while telling the scenery she was free.

I willed myself not to take her back right there—take her where she would never be found again.

She had changed so much, it was almost like watching a stranger. The need, though…the burst of ownership, tore and fought to take back what belonged to me, but she wasn't alone. A baby cradled in a sling thing attached to her chest and waist kept me solidified to the shadows.

Then that fucker appeared, taking the child from her and putting his lips where mine should have been. His hands lowered onto the olive skin that had been exposed to too much sun, but she wasn't his to touch. He whispered words into her ear, eliciting a smile that should have only been for me.

Fuck him. He can have her smiles. I'll take her tears, her moans, her begging, and her pain.

Sweat beads on my shaven head, the branches of the tree offering little escape from the midday heat. My beard had grown in longer than I usually kept it, but the women appear to like the facial hair. It's a magnet for the sluts looking for a good time. It also attracts the females who like the rougher side of sex. The bitches begging me to inflict pain only angered me into doing so.

Sex is supposed to be an outlet, but it only made the beast inside roar for freedom.

There is no outlet for me without her.

The whores are not worthy. They are not satisfying. They are not *my* doll.

My pretty little doll.

The black rotting remains of my old house—*our* home—taunt me as the time passes slow and torturous.

The grounds are untouched.

Covered by wild growth, undisturbed, until now.

Old memories shift and sway within my mind, begging to take root and keep me imprisoned here.

There are ghosts that haunt me when I come back here. Yellow tape still lingers in some of the overgrown weeds from where the police dug up every inch of the grounds, taking what didn't belong to them.

Disturbing the past.

Thoughts of my father push into the forefront of my mind—his betrayals. I hate that I can't get to him to end his miserable fucking existence.

I've heard prison for a cop is brutal, but based on whose terms?

I can think of worse ways he should suffer.

He *deserves* to suffer—to live in the hell he created.

Distant reverberations of an engine coax a change in the atmosphere.

The air shifts around me, almost welcoming the emotion that comes with seeing her. My soul cries out, begging her to speak to me. I need to hear her, feel her, be inside her.

I need to find the peace again—the peace she brought me when she didn't run, didn't betray me, didn't fucking kill me.

My life since her has been an awakening. Finding Tanner changed everything for me, but still, her presence, or absence of it, lingers in my daily thoughts.

Three Years Ago

My father always made sure I was prepared when the time came I'd need to make changes—the time to get away. Being who I was came with consequences and risk.

Pulling myself from the grass, my skin protests, shrinking over my bones. I'm a mess, and I need help.

Seeking it out irks me, but my life just disintegrated in front of my eyes—literally.

My father was compromised, so going to this place could lead me into cuffs matching his, but it's a gamble I'm going to have to take. I have nowhere else. There shouldn't be any reason why my father would give them an asset, and according to my father, that's what this person is.

I begin walking a couple miles west from where my home once stood and venture just into the brush where the tree is carved with a letter B. Eventually, I locate the rock marked with a small indentation of the same letter, and I set to removing it from the dirt. The chill in the air nips at the exposed, torched flesh on my arm and shoulder. The gunshot wound is nothing in comparison to smelling your own skin cook. My body shakes without permission, my eyes clouding as I dig, my nails splitting as I scratch at the dry dirt.

Relief coaxes a sigh from my lips when the leather handle from the satchel strokes the tips of my fingers. Yanking it free, I collapse, breathing hard.

I need water.

Gathering the strength to sit up, I pull the zipper and look inside. Bills stacked in bundles of thousands stare back at me.

Thirty thousand won't suffice for the long term, but it's a start.

The card sitting on top makes my skin vibrate.

I'm not used to needing people or having to rely on them, but times are changing. This change has been forced upon me by my dirty little doll.

The burner cell has the number already saved inside and the card simply reads: **TANNER**

One hand hits dial while the other grips the grass, squeezing until my damaged fingernails cut into the palm.

The dial tone ticks, then it's ringing.

Ring.

Ring.

Ring.

"What name do you have?" a woman asks.

"Tanner," I croak back, the damage to my body taking its toll.

"Please hold."

Fucking music plays down the line.

What the hell?

I stand alone, a voice croons, *surrounded by guitar riffs. How ironic the lyric is to me.*

The music cuts off and a male voice comes over the line.

"Where are you?" His tone is deep and calm. He speaks with a manner akin to that of friends having a casual catch up call. "I'll send a car to pick you up, but I need to know where you are."

"I'm two or three miles from my house…"

The call drops before I can give him the address.

I don't like it, but my body is weakening and the darkness of night steals my consciousness.

My mind swims in lucid dreams as voices chase away the flames wrapping around my body.

Water drips, pulling me from the hold of sleep.

Drip.

Drip.

Drip.

My eyes spring open, and I jerk forward. Water laps around me, splashing.

I'm in a tub.

"Calm down," a voice orders. It's the same tone from the call.

There's authority in his manner, and I find myself stilling and taking in my new surroundings. Dark tiles cover the walls to the ceiling. A large mirrored wall dominates the space. I'm sitting naked inside a huge corner bath. The water is murky and cool to touch.

My eyes draw to the man standing over me, studying me.

He's tall and wears a suit and tie. A fancy fucker.

Is he going to take me on a goddamn date?

What the hell?

Who is this guy?

Pain radiates over my entire back, stealing my breath.

The man, Tanner, continues to simply watch me.

His hair is dark and thick, neither long nor short, pushed backwards out of his face. His eyes look like the color of the flames I just escaped from.

His thick lips curl into a smirk.

"I didn't think I'd ever meet you," he announces, as if he knows who and what I am. "Your father has accumulated quite a few favors owed."

He stares with a subtle nod of his head, not yet knowing my father can't offer any more of those "favors"—not from where he is now.

Would that prevent him from helping me if he knew?

Fuck it. It's irrelevant. I'll be gone soon, finding my own way like I always have.

"The doctor is due back any minute," he assures me. "She will dress your burns. The bullet from your shoulder has already been removed, and she's done her best to prevent scarring, but some is inevitable, I'm afraid. I hope you're not a vain man."

His eyelashes lower as his head tilts to one side. Curious amber eyes penetrate mine.

"Why are you staring at me?" I growl, feeling more exposed than I ever have before—and it has nothing to do

with being naked.

He's not eyeballing me in a way you would someone you want to fuck. It's something else…wonder, maybe? Shifting on his feet, he lowers himself to sit on the side of the tub and dips his hand into the water, letting the liquid run through his fingers.

"I'm admiring you. You're quite extraordinary, and I'm looking forward to helping you harness your full potential. You're not alone anymore." His voice holds a surety I'm not used to. "We're going to be great friends, Benny."

The rumbling of an engine vibrates through the air and my heart rattles, dragging me back to the present.

Coming to a stop, I recognize the model of Dillon's shit heap tin can of a car. Forcing myself lower, I push against the bark of the tree concealing me. The old scars scream in protest, and I let the pain anchor me to this moment.

My scars are a constant reminder of my dirty little doll and her betrayal.

They are the birthmark of the new man reborn from the flames she engulfed me in.

My hand twitches with the fleeting need to kill—her, him, me. But I never see it through, and I can't determine why. It's been years since she was mine, and her absence leaves me lonely in a way no one else can fill.

She belongs to me.

She will always belong to me.

I don't see enough of her, following her, watching her. I need to bask in this moment, commit everything to memory for a later time—a reminder to myself she's not the dirty little doll sculpted by my hand anymore.

She's been ruined...*by him.*

The passenger side door opens and jean clad legs belonging to the girl I used to know step out. She bends down and mumbles something through the window, but I can't make out what she says. It's just a murmur of a sound, no structure to it. Her hair ripples with her forceful strides as she pushes her legs to move through the thick brush, fighting her way through to get to her destination.

This place is a forgotten graveyard to her, but to me, it's home. Me. Us.

Rage sizzles under the surface, battling with need, sorrow, and disappointment.

She comes to a stop, her chest heaving. The swollen belly full of another life that's not mine protrudes and ridicules me.

I could move quick and end it all here and now. Take her life, then my own. What a perfect *fuck you* that would be to that dickhead who thinks I'm long gone.

But with the new her, comes new changes for me also.

I'm not the same man I used to be.

I don't act irrationally. I think every step through.

The sun dances over the new red in her hair.

I hate it.

She doesn't need to dye her hair. It looks unnatural and cheap. She's heavier around her hips, her frame thicker. Motherhood has changed her body—*he* changed my perfect doll so much. I fucking hate that cunt pig. I should peel his skin from his body and wear him while I fuck the me back into her.

Her sigh is loud and carries to me, sending chills up my spine. Her eyes are on the charred remains of what was once our life, but mine are on her from a small gathering of brush next to a tree far enough back; she wouldn't notice it among the others unless she were seeking it out.

My focus moves to the car out of her sight.

Dillon, the fuck face, has gotten out, his cell phone attached to his ear. It would be so simple to take him by surprise, creep up behind him, slit his throat, and paint the asphalt crimson.

I could coat my doll's hair in real red—blood red.

My cock jerks and stiffens at the thought.

The rolling down of the back window gains my attention, chasing a shiver up my spine. Little fingers appear, and my heart races.

Thud.
Thud.
Thud.

They have the child with them. Grabbing the little dolly from the gift I plan to leave here for my dirty doll, my head swims with the need to see the child.

My body dips behind the long, overgrown grass, moving through it like a deadly snake. The stupid so-called detective has moved a good twenty feet, pacing and shaking his head as he rants to someone about not doing their job right. He's the king of not doing his job right.

My stomach tightens as I approach her window while remaining aware of Dillon's distance and view of the car.

A smile bright and innocent beams at me through the gap in the window.

Brown eyes with a hint of green stare into my own,

thick lashes batting like dragonfly wings.

"Dwink?" she coos, holding out a cup with a nipple looking thing on the end.

"You look just like your mommy," I murmur in awe.

She giggles, holding her arms out to me.

I could just take her. I wonder how far I would get.

What punishment that would be for my dirty doll.

Instead, I bestow my gift, and fade away while she's distracted, back to my shadow, letting the racing of my heart pump the adrenaline through my veins. A smile graces my dirty doll's lips, but drops as she studies the scene around her. Her body visibly shivers, then a horn pierces the air, drawing her eyes. She moves away, and I hear her car door close.

I tighten my grip on the knife I've taken from my bag.

Waiting.

Anticipating.

The melody flows through the air, and I hum the words as the dolly sings.

Miss Polly had a dolly who was sick, sick, sick,
So she phoned for the doctor to be quick, quick, quick.
The doctor came with his bag and his hat,
And he knocked at the door with a rat-a-tat-tat.
He looked at the dolly and he shook his head,
And he said, "Miss Polly, put her straight to bed!"
He wrote on a paper for a pill, pill, pill,
"I'll be back in the morning yes I will, will, will."

My palm sweats around the handle of the knife clutched so tight, it becomes a part of me. The engine coughs, then rumbles as it departs. They didn't come looking. They didn't think it was me.

PRETTY NEW DOLL

How could it be a gift from me?

I don't exist anymore.

A soft moan comes from below me, hair flaying over the top of my boot.

Eyes, wide and panicked, stare up at me, her head moving back and forth—no, no, no.

Yes. Yes. Yes.

Reaching down, I grasp her cheap hair in my other hand, lifting her weight effortlessly from her broken position. She'd been out longer than I'd thought she would be. She was all wrong to be my doll—crude with her tongue and loose with her cunt.

Breathing in through my nose, I let the high have its moment, then plunge the knife down into her chest. It slides in like penetrating a tough steak, one that's more rare than cooked. Squealing around the gag in her mouth, she shakes her body back and forth, her arms pulled and tied tight around her back. The second blow, followed by the third, brings her body to more of a tremble, her fight waning.

Straddling her small frame, I dip my head to hers, my nose almost touching her lips. Fear has a unique scent, and when death is so close, you see its company in their eyes. It's beautiful being on the cusp of life and death with them, feeling their body jerk and strain as it drags in its final breath and expels it with their soul.

When she stills, I swipe my hand through the blood adorning her chest and paint her lips.

Images of the little girl and the gift I gave her just moments before play out in my thoughts.

I hold up the doll and poke my hand through the

window. The child grabs the doll, her slobbery little finger brushing against my own.

"Dolly," she gurgles, dribble coating her fat bottom lip.

"Yes. It's a dolly." I grin down at her, much like I did her mother many years ago. "A pretty doll for a pretty little doll."

CHAPTER ONE

~ *Unknown* ~

Benny

Pushing through the club doors, I nod to the bouncer. They all know me as Tanner's friend here at The Vault. If you're a friend of Tanner, nobody gives you any shit. A blonde with a sultry smile bats her lashes at me as I walk past, but I'm not interested. She's not offering anything I'm buying, and she doesn't realize how lucky that makes her.

My tastes are unique.

Peculiar.

Anomalous, as Tanner always says. Whatever the fuck that means.

Regardless, Blondie, with her big fake tits and whore outfit, is *not* my type. Maybe if I were in the mood to strangle her ass. But I'm not. I'm in the mood to fuck away the thoughts of my dirty doll holding another life inside her that isn't mine. To fuck away the anger, sorrow, disgust.

Stalking through the club, I head straight for the VIP room Tanner always seems to have reserved. I've never asked him because our relationship isn't like that, but I think he owns this club among many more. After he found me, he brought me back here. Told me this place was my playground. To ask, and I shall receive.

I've been asking, though, and he can't seem to deliver what I want.

That's because I want *her*.

And nothing in this world comes free.

Anger bubbles in my chest once again as thoughts of the pretty little doll I let get away simmer in. Not a day goes by where I don't obsess over her. Sometimes, I imagine a scenario where she and her baby dolly are mine. A family, if you will. But reality seeps in, ruining my goddamned fantasy.

Being in the outside world has changed me. I've been made aware of rules I never cared for or abided by, but keeping my profile low is how I will get what I want in the end. So, for now, I mostly obey. Patience is key to not reacting in the moment and doing something stupid that will get me killed or locked up with Daddy Dearest.

I can't get her.

Not yet.

I may be psychotic, but I'm not stupid. Detective Shit for Brains has a constant eye on them both. I must plan and prepare.

"Benjamin," a deep, familiar voice rumbles as I push past the crimson velvet curtain leading to the fancy VIP room he's no doubt lounging in. The first time Tanner had made the mistake of calling me by my nickname, Benny, he saw the fire in my eyes and before I could even speak, he shut me down, calling me Benjamin from then on. It was unspoken, but at my weakest moment, it was as though he saw inside my mind while I sat in that cold bathtub.

"You're a new man, Benjamin. Stronger and more powerful, in control. You beat death—torn from the womb you lived in all those years. That house was suffocating you. Keeping you as its prisoner. The man you are is becoming the beast you were meant to be. Freed from his cage and released from his shackles, he's able to roam and feed as he sees fit. Benny is dead. Benjamin has risen."

I'd been ready to slit the creepy fucker's throat, but, of course, he preempted that as well. It's as if Tanner is always three steps ahead of me. When I stopped thinking of ways to murder him, he began to educate me. No longer hidden away in the safety of my home, I was vulnerable to many unseen threats. He showed me how to live like the monster I am—in plain sight.

Tanner has many friends in high places who all want something only he can deliver, and when the time comes he needs something in return?

Tit for tat, Tanner always says with a wicked grin and glint in his eye.

He doesn't have many people he spends time with barring me, though.

We are lone wolves who crossed paths under a new moon, and a bond formed I never thought possible.

I have a friend.

"Come, my friend," he instructs, pushing a pretty naked brunette from his lap. She slips out of the VIP room without another word. He's wearing a suit—I swear, it's his goddamn armor—and holds a glass of dark liquid in his lazy grip, his normally fiery golden eyes dimmed by whatever the fuck he's on tonight.

Walking into the room, I take the plush armchair in

front of him, a glass of bourbon waiting for me next to it. Tanner always seems to know when I'm coming.

"How was Amy?" he asks, and sips his liquor, a brow lifted in question.

I cringe at the thought of Amy—another one of Tanner's gifts. His gifts are never the ones I want. They seem to check off some of my criteria, but never enough. Not once has he brought me a woman who meets everything on my list.

That's because my pretty little doll is the only one who ever could.

And I think he knows it. She sated the deepest of my cravings.

"By the murderous scowl on your face, I take it she was unsatisfying." He smirks. "Hmmm? Did she disappoint you?"

I clench my jaw and run my palm across my buzzed scalp. I'm not sure how I feel about this new look, but Tanner says it's a must, changing my appearance every six months or so. And for some fucking reason, I trust this guy. He hasn't failed me yet.

"You could say that," I grunt.

He chuckles and sets down his glass. "We can't have that, now can we? What was wrong this time? Not young enough? Hair not dark enough? Pussy not tight enough?"

All fucking three.

And not my dirty little doll.

Pretty little doll.

I think about how beautiful Amy was when she bled out all over the forest floor. "She just wasn't...*enough*," I admit with a huff.

"What did you do with the body? Make a big fucking mess like last time?"

This time, I'm the one smirking. So, he's had to help me out of a few binds when I lost my head. "I took care of her. Shallow grave, but she's not going anywhere."

I left her as a big fuck you to my dirty doll and her man guard. The site she goes to mourn me is the cemetery of broken dollies.

And they call themselves detectives?

Well, fuck you both.

Leaning back in his chair, he narrows his eyes at me. "You know I love a challenge. Which is why…" his hand goes in the air and he snaps three times, "I have a surprise for you."

Childlike music begins to play, much like you'd hear from a jewelry box or at a carnival, and the curtain opens. A young woman steps into the room, and my dick immediately hardens in my jeans.

She's small…just like I like them.

Tiny tits.

Short pink dress.

Fullest fucking lips I've ever seen, but goddamn, at least they're real.

Big blue eyes, but they're too close together.

I curl my lip in disgust. The eyes are all wrong. My cock shrivels at the sight. Yet, she walks over to me shyly, her fingers tugging at the hem of her short dress.

"Sit on Monster's lap," Tanner orders, his voice icy cold. Everyone, including me, yields to him when he takes that tone. This girl, she nods her head in agreement. "Yes, Master."

Monster and Master.

Tanner says we're unique. Nobody is like us. We're a team. It took some time to trust him, but now I believe him.

The girl is hesitant, but straddles my thighs. Her palms skim up the front of my fitted T-shirt to my shoulders.

"Close your eyes," I snap, my own voice harsher than Tanner's.

She stiffens but obeys. *Good doll.* I let my palms roam over her small ass before sliding her dress up to her hips. When my hands slip back down, I find her bare underneath. Irritation blooms inside me. Good dolls wear lacy panties. They aren't whores like Blondie out front.

"Where are your panties?" I demand, my palm slapping her ass hard enough to make her cry out.

She jerks her head over her shoulder to look at Tanner. He simply shrugs and motions for her to turn back around. "Don't look at me, little doll. He's the one pulling your strings here."

Tanner's eyes darken as he watches fear blossom in hers.

She must sense the devil inside me, whispering all the ways to slice her, to prolong the bleeding, revel in her tears. Her eyes find mine again, distress dancing in the light blue ocean of them. Her terror has my dick getting hard again. Maybe I *can* work with this.

"Suck my cock, doll," I seethe as I shove her onto the floor. The thump as her body falls to a heap at my feet heightens my arousal.

My need to hurt has grown with my rage and sorrow over the years. The man they *killed* had a fetish, I know that now. But the man they created in the ashes has a need—a dark, deep-rooted urge that can only be sated by feeding its hunger.

The doll snaps into action—the whores always do when money is involved—and eagerly unfastens my jeans while kneeling in front of me. With her head bowed and dark hair curtaining her face, she could almost pass for my pretty little doll. My dick aches for relief. I grip the side of her hair, ignoring her yelp of surprise, and pull her to my cock as it jerks in her hand.

I can feel Tanner's eyes on us. His eyes are everywhere. Always watching. Always critiquing. Always aiding me when shit gets to be too much. I'm not sure why he's befriended me, but I can't say I'm bothered by it. It's nice to have someone who sort of understands me.

The pretty fake doll starts sucking on my thick cock as if she's done it a thousand times. Maybe she has. Tanner has whores on tap for the front of the club—the tame shit used as a façade for what he really offers. You have to be on his radar to know how to request the darker side of his world. Once, a man came in and asked for Robert. Tanner greeted him, and later, I asked why the man called him Robert, since that isn't his name. He said to me, he is Tanner. To that man, he is Robert. To Lucy, his bar manager, he is Cassian. Fuck knows what name is real, if any, and that's what keeps him safe. Anonymous.

The suckling on my cock brings my attention back to the dick loving doll. Her terror is long gone as she attempts to draw pleasure from me. So fucking eager. It irritates me rather than turns me on, and my cock starts to soften.

When her blue eyes lift, looking up at me in question

at my cock growing more flaccid by the second, I fucking lose it.

"You're a worthless doll," I snap, my hand seizing her throat. I yank her tiny frame up into my lap, my grip becoming deadly as the stupid bitch scratches at my wrist.

Tanner, ever the loyal friend, doesn't say a word in protest. He watches me, his gaze narrowed and a half smile playing at his lips.

The worthless doll's face turns pink, then red, until it's a beautiful dark purple as she frantically gasps for air. She should have asked what I wanted rather than being a money hungry whore. This is the first one who's had even a sliver of potential.

When I release her neck, tears pool and fall from the sea of her eyes. Holding her throat, she wheezes, trying to take in air.

"Bastard," she spits out, her tone venomous.

Little wrong doll has balls.

But mine are so much fucking bigger.

Shoving her back to her knees, I grip her head, urging my cock back into her mouth. I push in so deep, she chokes and gags and fights to be free. When her teeth clamp down, I smile. Little bitch.

Forcing her backwards, I straddle her shoulders and wrap one hand around her tiny neck while using the other to support my position on top of her.

Squeezing her neck, I pound my cock down her throat. Her body jerks and trembles beneath me, her mouth trying to open wider to gasp in breath, keeping her from being teeth happy.

Dying.

I fuck her face with all the power I can muster, thrusting my hips and squeezing her neck until a crunch gives under my hand. Her body goes limp at the crushing of her windpipe, and with it, my release tightens my balls. Heat builds, spreading through my groin up my back as I pull from her mouth and ribbons of cum paint her wide-open dead eyes.

Lifting to a standing position, I grab her under the arms and raise her without effort. Her body sags in my grip, and it's the first time she's looked like a real doll. Stupid dead doll, just like all the rest.

Fucking disgusted by her, I throw her away from me, and her head hits the corner of the coffee table with a sick pop. She rolls onto the floor face first, and I stare, fixated on the way blood blooms from a wound on the back of her skull. It doesn't pump out like it would if she were still breathing. It's more of a seeping, like a ketchup bottle being knocked over with no lid.

Now, that…

That gets my dick hard.

Straddling her unmoving form, I smear my palm across the back of her head, then stroke my cock using her perfect blood as lubricant.

"That's it, Benjamin," Tanner praises. "Release that monster. Feed your urges."

His words thread themselves into my mind and pluck away at any shards of sanity I had left. This beast rages with need.

Dolly.

Dolly.

Pretty little doll.

I'll make her mine again.

I just need to *take* her.

No other doll will do.

My nuts seize up violently as I succumb to a desperate orgasm. It's been ages since I've had a satisfying climax. And now, I've had two in a row. I look down in awe as my cum spurts thick ropes across the back of her bloody head. I'm still staring down at her when Tanner kneels in front of me. He runs his finger across a stream of blood pouring down her cheek and holds it up to the light.

"You still want your old doll. No changing that, huh?" he questions, his gaze still on his bloody fingertip.

"Nope," I admit, irritation clutching at my chest. She's not my old doll; she's the *only* doll who has ever been enough.

"Perhaps you should go get *her*. She's what truly satisfies your monster. Correct?" His fiery amber eyes meet mine as he sucks the worthless doll's blood from his finger.

"She's the only one."

And he knows it.

I was good for a while, and knew the risk outweighed the outcome if I'd attempted to retake my dirty doll. Being gone was the best thing for me to start anew.

A fresh start.

The possibilities intrigued me for a while. The women he gifted were a distraction. But now, the need has become overwhelming, and I've found myself wanting to know everything my dirty doll has been up to. I know the compulsion to take her will become too strong to deny for much longer, and Tanner clearly knows it too.

He gives me a single nod. "Then go get her, Benjamin.

You deserve her. I'll make arrangements to house you both in a secure location, but you will need to erase Detective Scott. He will be an issue otherwise, and it needs to look like the accident we discussed. Once he's taken care of, you *will* allow her to grieve. That way, everyone around her will believe her letter she will eventually write to say she's left to escape the crushing memories of him."

Patience.

I must exercise patience.

As much as it fucking drives me crazy, I know he's right.

He grins and tilts his head to study me. He has been doing that for the last three years.

"Where will we go?" I ask, curious of where would be far enough away to hide the reality of her being taken, not just up and leaving.

"Oh, you aren't going anywhere, my friend. Nothing comes for free, and I'm afraid I don't want to part with you. I've become too fond of you to allow you to disappear on me. Wouldn't you miss me, Benjamin?"

Would I miss him? Not if I had my doll. But I'm out of resources to pull off taking my doll back, and Tanner has been a lifeline for me. If I need anything, he supplies it. Am I ready to go at it alone…again?

No.

"I would miss our time together," I admit, nodding to the dead doll covered in my cum.

A burst of heavy laughter comes from Tanner's chest. "Indeed." Then he jerks his head away. "Wilson," he bellows to the guy standing guard in front of the red drapes. "Call for a full clean-up of one."

The dead dolly will soon be disintegrating in a bucket of acid.

It's been a few days, but Tanner's words play on repeat in my head. *"Then go get her, Benjamin. You deserve her."* I've somehow convinced myself to stay away all this time. I had plenty of excuses.

Someone might recognize me.

I might get caught.

Where would I take her?

Worst yet, what if she doesn't excite me anymore?

Without my pretty little doll as my purpose, I cease to exist. I'm a man who desperately craves something that isn't real. Something that isn't tangible. But what if I see her and those feelings wash over me once again? All encompassing. So fully.

"Then go get her, Benjamin. You deserve her."

There's no more putting it off. Tanner is making sure I have somewhere for just us two. Safe. Secure.

Which is why I've been following her the past few days. It's almost time. I watch as she takes her toddler to daycare. I watch as she heads to the police station for work. I watch as she works cases in the field. And I watch as she and that dick of a husband come home together each night as a family. They're all fucking smiles as they cook dinner and feed their family.

Each night, I've gone home more and more furious. I have no goddamn plan, but I want Dillon to suffer—suffer in a way that needs to look accidental.

She will mourn him, but only until I'm back inside

PRETTY NEW DOLL

her and she realizes once more he was never meant to touch her. She belongs *with* me. *To* me. It's always been *me*.

I'm on autopilot following her, so much so, I almost whiz past when she puts on her blinker to turn into a neighborhood that certainly isn't hers. A smirk plays on my lips. Her loser husband probably can't satisfy her. She's probably sleeping with some dumb motherfucker I will kill the moment she leaves.

Or maybe even seeing a lawyer to get a divorce.

Now, that idea puts a full-blown grin on my face.

But the moment I take in *where* she's stopping, my smile falls.

Why is she here?

This is my dad's old house before he was taken to prison. The house he shared with his new wife. The wife he took after he made my mother go crazy. He never brought me here, but I read about the pretty doctor, wife of the shamed, disgraced chief of police. Tanner was the one who gave me the address. He told me to seek out the woman and kill her if it would give me closure for my mother. Revenge.

But I didn't need to seek revenge in her honor. She didn't fucking deserve it. She took my Bethany away from me. Maybe if she hadn't, my life would be completely different.

I'd be different.

No, fuck the doctor *and* my mother.

I drive past the house, but don't take my eyes off my pretty little doll as she pulls her kid from the car. By the time the front door opens, I'm turned around and parked a few houses down. My pretty little doll is still fooling with the car seat when a girl walks down the steps toward them.

Bethany?

Thud.

Thud.

Thud.

Time slows as she bounds toward my pretty little doll.

Her long brown hair kicks up with the wind. She doesn't smile. The somber look on her face is exactly my sister's.

But not really my sister—*my Bethany*.

Did Dad hide her, heal her, fix her, and keep her from me all along?

No.

No.

No.

I saw her dead. I fucking buried her body. This is a trick. With a snarl, I pull the cell Tanner insisted I needed from my pocket and click on the camera, zooming in all the way.

Bethany shields her eyes from the late afternoon sun that's beginning to set. She's wearing a floral print dress that's short and makes her appear younger than I presume she is. It suits her tiny frame. My entire body thrums with excitement and fear. A mix of elation and confusion stir and battle inside me. Her features are small, and a gasp escapes me when visions of seven-year-old me cloud my thoughts.

My sister, Bethany, who was brutally taken by my father when I was so young, and my new Bethany my mother stole the light from. This girl is a beautiful combination of them both.

How is this possible?

After all this time, she's come back to me. Dad lied to me when he said he was replacing Bethany. She was never gone. He was always a sick, selfish bastard and kept her to himself.

My dirty little doll hands her child off to my Bethany, then she's back in the car, driving off.

And me?

I'm staring at the past, the present, the miracle.

I watch as she goes inside and attempt to wait patiently, which lasts about forty-five minutes. Before I go fucking crazy with anticipation, I climb out of my car and stride over to the tree line at the side of the house.

Thud.

Thud.

Thud.

I make sure to slip along the edge undetected until I'm at the side of the house, using the newly fallen dusk as my cover.

Latching onto the side garage door, I twist, testing it out, and to my delight, it opens. Slipping inside the garage is easy. When I reach the door leading inside the house, I am more careful. The door opens a crack, just enough for me to peek in.

Standing in the kitchen, with her back to me, is Bethany, stirring something on the stove. I open the door a little more, and the sounds of *Sponge Bob* carry through from another room. A little girl is singing the theme song.

Why is my Bethany babysitting my dirty little doll's child?

Bethany starts to turn, so I quickly pull the door shut and press my ear against the wood, listening to her bustle around the kitchen. Once it's quiet, I push it open again.

She's no longer in the kitchen, so I take the moment to slip inside. Peering around the corner, I find her in the dining room, her dark hair still hiding her face as she sets some silverware out on the table. The toddler is sucking on her juice, her body dancing to the cartoon music. I hide back around the corner and use the mirror on the wall cattycorner from her to see her.

"Eat up all your macaroni, MJ, and we'll go play dress up," Bethany says. I don't remember her voice being so soft and childlike. Something about it scratches away inside me. It's better than I remember. The toddler squeals with excitement and starts eating her food.

Bethany's head turns as she looks at the clock, giving me an unobstructed view of her face. Same pert nose. A smattering of freckles on her cheeks. Full, perfect lips. Wide hazel eyes, a perfect blend of brown and green. She's my two favorite Bethanys all wrapped into perfect doll-shaped form.

My cock hardens almost instantly.

I've missed all the Bethany girls Dad brought and later took from me. But the one I missed most of all was the one standing as a perfect replica inside this house.

I rub at my dick as I stare at her perfect form reincarnated. She's beautiful. I've loved and ached for her for so long…and now, she's finally here.

My phone starts buzzing in my pocket, and I freeze. Bethany's brows furrow as she listens, but I'm already back-stepping into the garage so I don't get caught.

Slipping out the side door, I haul ass back to my car. Once inside, I can't stop my beating heart.

Thud.

Thud.

Thud.

She's here.

I've missed a call from Tanner and one text.

Tanner: Where are you?

I scrub at my face before responding to my friend.

Me: I found my Bethany.

Three dots move before he replies.

Tanner: As in your sister?

Tanner knows some of my past, but only the bits I chose to share.

Me: Yes.

The Bethany girls who came and went were not really my blood sisters. They were given her name and title of sister, and it made me feel less alone in the empty world. This is the real one.

Tanner: Reaching out seems like a bad idea. I don't want to lose my friend because he did something irrational. Remember, you're free now. Don't let them cage you again. Planning is key in everything you do.

I smile because I'm fucking ecstatic. He's right, though. I can't just barge in, tell her I'm her brother and she belongs to me, then take her.

At least…not yet.

I need to make her a home first.

Then, I'm coming back for my sister.

My Bethany.

My perfect new doll.

Me: You're right. I won't fuck up.
Tanner: Of course you won't, Benjamin.

With my gaze on her house, which seems to shine like a beacon in the dark, I unzip my fly. Out comes my aching cock into my eager hand, and I stroke myself furiously as I watch her move in front of the windows.

I've found her.

I've fucking found her.

Tanner always said there was a reason I survived. A plan was in place for me, I just needed to be patient. He was right. She's been out here waiting for me to find her. And I did.

I climax hard with Bethany on my mind, and it makes me feel dirty and euphoric all in the same breath. Mama said I couldn't be with her like that. But we *did* want that. Bethany wanted that more than anything, and I won't let her down again. It's only when I see my dirty little doll's car return that it hits me.

I didn't follow her.

I didn't think about her.

I didn't fucking obsess over her.

I didn't want her.

The need and anger evaporated when Bethany came out of that house.

For the first time in all the years since knowing my dirty little doll, taking her, and loving her, my thoughts didn't dwell on her. The ache that intensified with each passing day ebbed, and I felt free. More free than I ever have.

Bethany is back, and the need to see her overruled the need to follow my dirty little doll.

I smile. How could I not?

My thoughts are clouded with Bethany when Lucy, the bar manager for Tanner's club, brings me over another drink. Her blonde hair is pulled into a sleek ponytail. Lucy is tall and has nice tits, but she's not my type. She always lingers around me, poking the blade of her knife into the bar surface, even knowing what and who I am. Any other woman would shrink away, but not her. She's not your typical woman, though.

She's a sadist. Obsessed with her fucking knives.

The bitch kind of reminds me of that blonde little psycho from the *Kill Bill* movies Tanner made me watch. Uma Thurman, maybe? Slender and slight but mean as fuck.

"I have something else for you." She smirks before sliding my drink on the table and handing me a notepad.

"What's this?"

"Some websites that may be to your liking. I have a new contact who offers something I think you'd like." She winks, then saunters off to help a customer.

Why she would go out of her way to think about my fucking needs has paranoia rearing its ugly head.

Everyone has a price, and if she thinks I'm going to let her open me up with her knife play and be her plaything, she has another thing coming.

She had been obsessed with my scars and pain threshold, and offered everything and anything for me to be her sub for a day. Bitch is crazy if she thinks she could ever get me to bow to her.

I flick through the notes, and curiosity beckons me to my computer.

"I'll keep looking for information on your sister," Tanner promises as he walks into my small office and picks up a notebook on my desk. "There was no mention of her in the papers when your father was arrested." I've been given a new ID, an office, and a job title for all intents and purposes.

Thanks to Tanner.

Always thanks to Tanner.

"What's this?" He starts flipping through the notebook.

I jerk it from his grip and scowl. "It's nothing."

His eyes are liquid fire as his nostrils flare. "Are we not friends?"

I clench my jaw and crack my neck. "We are."

Plucking the notebook from my grip, he flips through it again before staring at some websites that have been recently written down.

"These are all terrible," he grunts.

"I know," I agree. "I'm still looking for good ones."

Grabbing a pen, he scribbles out a site. "This one is new. It's not easily found because they offer some kinky shit most of the world can't handle. Use that log in and have at it."

Until I get my Bethany, I need to satisfy the urges clawing at me from the inside out. I'm conflicted and confused. My pretty little doll has been my focus for so long, but now...

"Let's have a look," Tanner says. "There's one in particular I think you'll like. I found her last night and have made a few inquiries." He licks his lips, tapping his finger on the side of the laptop in front of me.

I pull up the website, then scoot away so he can type in what he's searching for: *Pretty New Doll.*

My dick is hard again. And when a site pulls up, lust simmers throughout my nerve endings.

PrettyNewDoll is her screen name. My stomach lurches.

Pretty New Doll just like my pretty little doll…

Wavy red hair sits on top of her head, accentuating her fair features. Her dresses are perfect and appear to be hand sewn, making pride thump in my chest. And as I scroll down, I'm elated to discover pictures of her bending over, revealing white lacy panties.

A perfect doll.

Aside from the ugly ass hair, everything about her is perfect.

She wears long eyelashes that hide the color of her eyes, but it works for me too. I can get off by looking at this doll. She's petite, smooth, perfect.

"Apparently she does live feeds sometimes, but not sexual, just teasing. The entire fet community is into this girl. I was handed the link to the site last night. No matter what kind of fetish they prefer, and even though she doesn't do the sexual stuff—*yet*—everyone is obsessed with her." He grins wickedly. "I was going to get a price and save her for you. Pull some strings to see if I can get her for you. Everyone has a price. But since you're impatient, this will have to do for now," Tanner tells me. "What do you think?"

"I want her."

He chuckles. "Of course you do, friend. And you shall have her. Let me see what I can find out about her. As far as we know, she could be in fucking China."

Cracking my neck again, I lean forward to admire her porcelain skin. "Then we track her down. Wherever she is, I want her."

He clutches my shoulder. "We'll find her. In the meantime, I need you to do me a favor."

I nod while flipping through her pictures. Tanner asks for favors from time to time, and they're never anything I can't handle. If I'm honest, I enjoy the fuck out of doing him favors.

Pulling a picture from his pocket, he slaps it on the desk. "Address is on the back. Make it happen. Tonight."

Pretty New Doll will have to wait.

But not for long. Soon, I will have her *and* my sister. Life will be perfect again. Flipping to a clean section of my notebook, I start scribbling down everything I'll need to build a cell to house my objects of affection—one much better than the one I had before. When I finish, Tanner rips it from the notebook and stuffs it in his pocket.

"You scratch my back and I scratch yours. Tit for tat," he says before walking away without another word.

In Tanner-speak, he'll get me my shit if I get him what he wants.

I stand and grab my hoodie. On the way out, I swipe my knife.

I'm amped and ready to shed some blood.

Tanner's favors are fun.

CHAPTER TWO

~ *Unspoiled* ~

Dillon

I'VE SEEN PLENTY OF CRIME scenes, been a part of a couple, but none have made bile form in my throat quite like this before.

Is that a fucking dick I'm staring at?

Who the hell did this poor, chopped-up motherfucker piss off?

"What do we have?" I raise my chin to a uniform I don't know.

He offers me a face mask, and I snatch it to cover my nose.

"Homicide," he spouts.

No fucking shit homicide, Sherlock. No one can do this to their self or claim it was an accident.

"Sorry, he slipped and landed on my knife while I was making shish kababs. I didn't notice he wasn't chicken until he was in pieces."

Fucking idiot.

I give him my narrowed stare, which usually has the uniformed cops snapping to attention, but he just stands there gaping around like a fish out of water.

"And?"

"No sign of forced entry," he says slowly. "So, I'm assuming he knew the killer."

"You're not paid to assume, and you're treading all over my crime scene." I point to the bloodied flesh on his shoe.

Yanking his gaze down to his feet, his eyes widen and body jerks, then he's running toward a trashcan and emptying the contents of his stomach. The piece of flesh, which looks like an ear, is still stuck to the sole of his shoe.

"Stop fucking moving," I bellow.

"Someone bag the ear," Marcus yells, shaking his head as he saunters over to where I'm standing. "Neighbor didn't hear a thing. She said the guy's name is Maximus Law. He owns a club downtown called Rebel's Reds."

I know the place. It's a shithole for fucking sadists to get their rocks off.

"Rivalry?" I put out there. Club owners, especially in the seedier scenes, dabble in the criminal world and can get competitive.

"It was one hell of a grudge if it is." Marcus wrinkles his nose.

"This wasn't just a warning or message," I state. "Someone enjoyed dismembering the body. Drawing out the kill. There's blood covering every inch of this place."

"Is that his…?" Marcus trails off, looking down at the member on the floor.

"Yep," I utter. "Let's find the timeline leading up to the death and go from there."

Shaking the disturbed look from his face, he nods his head. "Already on it. CSI's here. Let's clear the scene."

Gladly.

"I want statements taken from everyone in this building. Someone has to have seen something, even if they don't realize they have," I bark at the uniforms now blocking the corridor.

"The club?" Marcus questions.

"Looks like it."

So much for catching the girls for dinner.

Pulling my cell from my pocket, I hit Jade's contact info and listen for the sweet sound of her voice.

Doesn't matter how many years pass, I still can't get enough of her. Just the sound of her voice placates my soul.

Ring.

Ring.

"Hey, babe," she breathes down the line, and I feel myself relax.

"How was your appointment?"

Six months pregnant and she's still refusing to slow down or hire a nanny.

She's been part-time at the precinct since having MJ, and not having her around all the time was hard to get used to, but knowing I get to go home to her and our baby every night was more than I ever thought I'd get. Life is good. Fucking good.

"It was fine. I'm on my way to pick up MJ now."

"How are the twins?"

"Elise is on campus, so it's just Elizabeth there," she says with a sigh. "She seems okay, but you never know with her."

"I'll check in on them this weekend," I offer, knowing she worries about the girls.

"Thank you. I know you're busy, but …"

"You don't need to thank me or explain. I care about them too, and it's not a problem."

Maryann, the twins' mother and Stanton's now ex-wife, has been doing a lot of traveling on top of her new busy schedule at the hospital. Medical conventions or some shit, and the girls are pretty much left to their own devices now that they are nineteen.

"Okay," she whispers, and my dick twitches thinking of her breathless and needy.

"I'm going to be late tonight, but try to stay awake for me, okay?"

"Mmmm," she agrees. "And if I am asleep, make sure you wake me."

Yeah, my girl is just as needy for me as I am for her. Fucking right I'll be waking her.

"Love you," I say before cutting the call. I ignore the shit-eating grin Marcus beams my way. I'm sure that fucker has been having his teeth whitened. He's around my age, but he's definitely a lot more suave than my rugged ass. I've seen Jade check out his ass a time or two when he takes off his suit jacket.

"You guys are so cute," he sighs, his lashes fluttering in a dramatic way.

A quick punch to his arm and the girly shit stops.

"You going to stop acting like a female, James, and get yourself a woman?"

Detective Marcus James found himself single last year after being with the same woman for nearly a decade. Long hours and not much time at home seeing to her needs sent her into the arms of some rich prick. He dropped her ass after a few weeks, but she came running back to Marcus with her tail between her legs. Too bad she didn't count on him shutting down all emotions and refusing to forgive her.

He threw himself even more into the job, but from my experience—and every other detective will say the same—you need someone to come home to, to wash away all the shit we have to witness and show us the good in the world so the bad doesn't infect and corrupt us.

"I'm actually seeing someone." He shrugs, opening the car door and punching the zip code into the sat nav.

What the fuck?

"Who, and since when?" Pulling into traffic, I glimpse at him a few times, waiting for him to spill the fucking beans. Every day I'm with this asshole, and not once has he mentioned a woman.

He lifts his hands in surrender. "It's really new and she's younger than me. I'm not sure where it's headed, but…"

"But what, motherfucker?"

"But it feels good. I feel good for the first time in a long time."

Well, if that doesn't make me grin like a fucking teenage girl. Who's the female now?

"How old is she?" I query.

"Twenty-five."

"That's a good age," I tell him. "A woman's sex drive peaks at twenty-five."

I feel his narrowed gaze burning a hole in the side of my head.

"What?" I bark.

"How the fuck would you know that?"

"I'm a detective. It's my job to know the important shit," I retort.

He bursts into a hearty laugh, which causes one of my own.

When the laughter settles, I ask, "So, what's her name?"

He smiles and flicks his eyes to me. "Lisa."

"We should do dinner some time," I tell him.

Marcus nods his head. "I think we should."

Well, that's a good sign. She must be a keeper.

The car slows, and I swing her into a parking space at the back of club Rebel's Reds. The red silhouette of a busty female blinks on and off above the entry.

"Original," Marcus snorts, lifting his eyes to the sign.

Opening the door, a heavy built man stands on the other side, greeting us with a glare.

"Membership card?" he grunts.

I flash him my badge and pin him with a smug stare. "I've got it right here."

He rolls his eyes and looks over at the bar before shouting, "Morris, pigs are here."

Have I traveled back to the nineties? I didn't think people called us pigs anymore.

Walking over to Morris, I briefly show him my badge before shoving it back in the pocket of my slacks. "You got somewhere we can talk?"

"The owner isn't in yet," he drawls, his eyes remaining on the bar he's wiping down with a cloth.

"He won't be coming in either," Marcus grinds out as he snatches the cloth from the guy and tosses it. "He's in about thirty pieces back at his place."

"W-What?" Morris sputters, now giving us his full attention.

"When was the last time you saw Mr. Law?"

He folds his arms over his chest and scrunches his brows together. "Last night. He left around two in the morning. He took one of the girls with him." He looks around the room. Half-naked women saunter around the place with old men dribbling in their chairs as they watch every motion, and naked girls wrap themselves around poles like it's part of their DNA. It's not that busy, but the atmosphere feels seedy and damp. The walls are dark gray with mirrored panels, white circular couches/beds sitting out in front of them. Everything looks like it's made of PVC. Easy cleaning. It's cheap, and doesn't warrant someone killing for rivalry.

"Scarlet," Morris calls out, and one of the many red-headed barmaids looks over, smacking her lips together. "Who left with Max last night?"

Rolling her eyes, she turns, calling over her shoulder, "One of the new stock. Jessica Rabbit, he called her. She looked like shit in my opinion."

New stock?

Morris's face blanches.

"He's buying women?" I question with a raised brow.

Morris shrugs. "I don't know anything about that. I just work the bar."

"Yeah right," I growl. "Where is Law's office?"

He fidgets with some glasses, keeping his head lowered, and Marcus slams his hand down on the bar. "Do you want us to shut this place down and take all your asses in for questioning?"

Morris jumps and lets out a rushed breath of air. "It's through the back. Code eight, one, six."

My gaze catches his eyes darting to the big asshole at the door. He's worried about what we'll find in Law's office, but he's more worried about being brought in, so we're getting away with not needing a warrant.

I follow Marcus through a door behind the bar. The walls down the corridor to the office are painted a deep red with pictures of old classic singers adorning them. There's a set of double doors to the right, and Marcus pushes through, sticking his head in.

"What the fuck?" he mutters as he waltzes inside.

I follow behind him and come to a stop. Crates—fucking dog crates with naked women inside. I count eight of them. Marcus immediately rushes over and tries to open them, but they're secured with padlocks. Thoughts of Jade and that sick fuck spring to mind, and my rage builds, rattling under the skin.

"Call it in," I bark before turning and stalking from the room.

Marching back through to the bar, I look around. Morris is nowhere to be seen. I push past the giant fuck at the door, and jog over to my car, popping the trunk and rummaging through for my bolt cutters. As I'm walking back through the doors of the club, the big guy opens his stupid mouth.

"They're paid for, pig. No laws being broken."

What a dumb motherfucker.

I fist my hand and swing, giving him a kidney shot. He bends over in pain, and I grab his sweaty, meaty head and bring my knee up to greet it. He rebounds off, collapsing to the floor. His size might be worth something to a club patron, but I come up against pieces of shit like him every day.

"Police brutality," he whines, holding his broken nose.

"You fucking tripped," I growl.

Marcus is on the phone calling for backup when I walk into the office, and all the girls are huddled at the doors of their crates. I snap the locks one-by-one, and each girl, timid and cautious, crawls out.

A couple of them look real young. Most likely still in their teens.

"It's okay. You're all safe." I placate them by showing my badge. "Can you tell me what you're doing here?"

Wide eyes stare up at me from a blonde girl. Her arms cover her tits and she's crossing her legs—not the usual stance of a hooker, which only tightens the pounding in my chest. These women are not here willingly. Maybe that Law fucker *did* deserve what he got.

"YA zaplatil za azartnyye igry moyego ottsa," the girl in front of me spews out.

What is that? Russian?

"I don't speak Russian," I tell her.

"Man bought me," she offers meekly with a thick accent.

And this investigation just got a lot more complicated.

"Get on the phone. Get a translator down here *and* Homeland Security."

"On it."

"And, Marcus," I continue as he looks over his shoulder at me, "close this goddamn place down."

Turning the key, darkness greets me in the corridor of our home. There's a small glimmer of light coming from the kitchen area, and a smile lifts the corners of my lips.

I know I'll find food and beer left out for me. Checking the time blinking at me from the oven, I sigh. It's well past one in the morning and I'm just getting home. I'm glad she didn't wait up for me. This pregnancy, like the last, isn't the easiest on her body. It's a miracle we conceive so easily with so much scar tissue on her cervix. Her pregnancies are higher risk, but damn if it's not worth it. There is nothing like seeing the woman you love carrying your child.

My thoughts go to the women we rescued tonight. They were all trafficked from Russia. Maximus had contacts with names and numbers written in a notebook, his finances all traceable. He was an amateur, and that is no doubt what got him murdered.

The circles he pushed himself into don't like loose ends or careless buyers. It's sloppy and gets criminals caught. I have more interviews to go through tomorrow with the staff, and hopefully the CCTV inside the club will give us some breadcrumbs to follow. Usually when a piece of shit like Maximus gets taken out, I wouldn't spend a sleepless night worrying about his killer. But the way he was mutilated and the circumstances of the trafficked women…I know this will lead to bigger fish and maybe saving more women. Human traffickers are the scourge of the earth, and bringing these fuckers down are worth all the sleepless nights it takes.

The smell of cooked meatballs causes a rumble in my

gut. Twisting the lid off a beer, I take a hearty gulp before devouring the food. I'm just rinsing my bowl when small hands wrap around my waist.

"I thought I heard you come in," Jade whispers against my back.

Turning in her arms, I pull her closer, a smile brimming my face when I see her Glock on the counter. She's a protective mama bear, and it's a turn on more than I'd care to admit.

"I'm sorry I woke you," I tell her, kissing the top of her head.

"I asked you to." She grins against my chest, her swollen stomach caught between us.

Pulling away, she tilts her head, looking up at me.

"Hey," she murmurs.

Damn, I love this woman. She's more relaxed this time round with her pregnancy, now that Benny is dead and she doesn't have that constant fear plaguing her that he will come for her, or worse, MJ. It's natural for her to have those feelings and even with him being gone, anxiety can cause old wounds to resurface.

A while back, MJ had been clutching onto some fucked-up doll that sang a song suddenly in the back of the car when we were doing our annual trip to his gravesite—the unmarked site where Jade burned him to the ground inside the prison he had kept her in.

We both almost shot the fucking doll, Jade accusing his ghost of fucking with her. It was almost comical if her terror wasn't so heartbreaking to witness. A quick call to my mother, though, put her mind at rest when she said she thinks she'd bought it for her last time she babysat. My mother is always buying her shit she doesn't need. Hell, we are *all* always buying her shit she didn't need.

"Hey, baby," I murmur, breathing her in.

"Tough day?"

"It was one of those days," I tell her, knowing she understands exactly what that means. She's had those days herself.

"Let me make it better." She bites her lip as her hands fumble with my belt. Then, she's unzipping my slacks and lowering to her knees.

Grabbing under her arms, I raise her up. "The floor is cold. Let me take care of you." I sure as fuck don't want my pregnant wife kneeling on the cold tile floor to suck my cock.

I lift her onto the counter and tug open her robe. She's bare beneath, her olive skin soft and creamy, her tits pert and begging for me to suck on them. I love the way her nipples darken when she's pregnant. Her swollen belly looks like she swallowed a small melon. I push gently on her shoulders, and she leans back on her elbows. Her cunt opens like a ripe flower as she spreads her legs for me, and wet excitement coats her pussy lips, making my mouth water.

Leaning down, I lap up her taste, teasing her clit with subtle flicks. Her hips jolt when I plunge my tongue inside her needy hole. My hands caress up her body and grasp onto her perfect tits, rolling the nipple between my forefingers and thumbs.

Her hips gyrate, and I know she needs me at her clit. I move my strokes over the throbbing bud and suck hard as I slip two fingers inside her. Curling them so the tips stroke her just right, I finger her until she's tightening around them, her pants loud and heavy.

"Right there…oh fuck, don't fucking stop," she gasps.

When her release floods around my fingers, it's the sexiest thing, and sends me into a frenzy. Every. Fucking. Time.

Pulling my face away, I line my dick up and push in with a firm thrust. Looping my arms around each thigh, I tug her ass off the edge of the counter and rock my hips into her. Her hands fondle her tits, making me harder than granite. I power my thrust into her vice-tight pussy, relishing the warm, wet release caressing my cock with each measured stroke.

This is exactly what I needed after a day like today.

My balls tighten with my fast approaching release, and just as I'm about to explode, I pull out and let the ribbons of cum spurt over her beautiful stomach.

We're both breathing heavy, sated and in need of a shower.

As if reading my mind, she pipes up, "Let's take a nice bath instead."

That sounds fucking perfect.

CHAPTER THREE

~ Strange ~

Benny

H E WAS A SCREAMER.
It fucking irritated me.

Fear is so much more thrilling when it's silent—in their eyes and the tremble of their flesh. The girl was unexpected, and her fear was perfect. She stood frozen, until the sight of me butchering whoever that man was to her became too much, causing her to faint. Her heaped form was a prize I didn't expect to return with, and usually I wouldn't have, but here I was and here she was.

The lock disengaging alerts me to Tanner's arrival. Other than me, he's the only one who has keys to my place—his place.

His heavy footfalls come to a stop beside me. His scent fills the air, and the atmosphere shifts when I sense he has seen the girl. She's a brunette, young, pretty, heavier set than I usually like them, but there was something about her silence when she first saw me, watched me kill that man, that intrigued me. She wasn't new to violence—death.

"Who is this?" Tanner asks, folding his arms and

studying the female asleep on my couch.

"She was at the apartment of the job you gave me."

I watch his brow furrow. "And you decided to take her with you?"

"It seemed like a waste to just end her there."

Tanner takes the few strides to where she sleeps and pushes her hair from her face. "She's pretty."

Yes, she is.

"You know the rules."

Yes, I do. We don't take or kill randomly. If she's missing and being looked for, it could lead to us.

"Wake her."

I pick up the drink I'd placed on the table moments before and launch the liquid at her sleeping form.

A gasp echoes through the apartment as she jerks into a sitting position. Her eyes widen when she sees me standing before her. Tanner moves to my side, and her pale green eyes flit to him, then back to me.

"Who are you?" Tanner asks in a smooth tone—one reserved for when he's being cautious and aloof.

"Dina," she answers in a thick accent, pronouncing her name DEEnah.

"What were you doing with Maximus?"

Her brows pull together at the mention of the dead man's name.

"The man you were with tonight," Tanner clarifies, leaning forward with an outstretched hand to tuck a strand of hair behind her ear.

"He owns me," she whispers.

"You were part of the shipment that came in?" His head tilts to the side as he studies her outline. She's wearing a tight black dress that barely covers her ass. She sits on bended knees, her arms resting at her sides. She doesn't flinch away from his touch.

"Yes."

"Your English is good?"

She shrugs her shoulders and nods her head in agreement. "My mother was English born."

"Your owner is dead," he casually comments.

Her green eyes snap to me, and she once again nods her head.

"Do you want to be free, Dina, or would you like a new master?" He strokes down her cheek before grasping her chin and bringing her eyes to his. Her chest begins to move in quick succession. Tanner slips his thumb into her mouth, exploring the warmth. Pulling free, he reaches down for the neckline of her dress. Taking it in both hands, he tugs. A rip pierces the air, and the fabric sags in ruins, exposing the flesh beneath. Her small, round tits have rosy pink nipples that match the color of her lips. Her rounded stomach holds a dusting of moles. She's not wearing panties, and just the V of her pussy is showing, the slit concealed between her closed legs.

"Did Maximus fuck you?" Tanner hisses in question.

She shakes her head no.

"Do you want to open your legs for me?" He poses it as a question, but it's laced with so much authority, it sounds like more of a demand. Even the most coy would find it hard to deny this man.

It is something I admire about him.

Shifting on the couch, she opens her legs.

Her cunt is as pink as her nipples. She has a flower

shaped clit, like a tulip sitting just outside the lips. She's been used a lot, and it shows in her demeanor and the opening of her cunt.

"I want to smell you. May I?" Tanner requests, but again, it's more of a statement. He gets the reaction he's used to: an eager, but not completely sure nod.

Dampness glistens between her thighs. She would never make a good doll, but I brought her here for this reason. To play with Tanner. A bonding of two monsters.

Tanner leans down on one knee and inhales between her thighs. "Are you a dirty, little slut who wants her pussy filled?" he breathes, closing his eyes before springing them open, the amber flames licking his pupils. "Would you like me to fuck you?"

She nods her head. Yes. Always yes.

"No," he snaps. "Use your words."

She glimpses at me, then back at Tanner, her face blushing crimson.

Tanner's broad laugh booms through the room.

"You want us both to fuck your dripping holes? What a dirty, whorish girl you are."

Gripping her wrist, he yanks her from the couch, and her body collides with his. "Monster, what hole would you like?" He spins so he's facing me and her back is to me.

"Ass," I bark.

A wicked grin spreads over his face.

His hand unfastens his suit trousers, releasing his hard, thick cock. He has more girth than I do, but I'm longer. With one hand, he manages to roll a condom down his length, sheathing himself from her nasty, most likely disease-riddled cunt.

"We don't know how many visitors this pussy has greeted," he sneers over her shoulder before tossing a condom at me.

Lifting her up his torso, her legs wrap around his waist before he forces her down on him. Her gasp of pain sends my blood sizzling through my veins. His hand grips her throat, forcing her chin up to look at him. "I want you to bleed. Do you want to bleed for me?" Tanner croons as he walks over to the couch and drops his weight down.

She bounces on top of him, crying out, "Yes."

Laying back, he releases her neck and loosens his tie before pulling it free. Finding my legs, I move into action. Taking the tie, I bind her arms behind her back, resting them on the bridge of her ass. My pulse quickens when she moves over him, grinding her hips.

Freeing my cock, I stroke over the lubricated condom as I pull it down my throbbing length. I peel my shirt off over my head and reach for the knife tucked safely in my boot before kicking them off, followed by my jeans.

Tanner's hands go back to her neck, tugging her down onto him so her ass is accessible to me. I take the knife and slice across her left wrist, then the right. The release of whooshing breath escaping her lips and jar of her body thickens my cock further. A crimson river forms down the crack of her ass and I find myself spreading her cheeks to coat the puckered hole.

"It hurts," she whines, trying to move off Tanner.

"Of course," Tanner groans. "All the good sex does." He tightens his grip on her throat, making her hiss.

Dipping my fingers in the blood now dripping between Tanner's legs and pooling on the couch where my knees rest, I paint my cock before ramming inside her tight asshole. She gargles and whimpers through the small airway Tanner is allowing, her fight fleeing as she continues to weaken from the blood loss. My cock feels every muscled ring stretch as I push past it.

"I can feel you," Tanner growls as I hammer my hips into her, the thin wall of flesh separating my cock from his offering a friction that feels incredible. The blood is everywhere, slapping between our pounding bodies and spraying a mural over her back. Her body sags over Tanner, her head lolling to the side with his hands neatly wrapped around her neck, holding her face to his.

"I can taste her dying," he pants, his wild amber eyes glowing with fire when they meet mine.

My heart thunders inside its cage and my head clouds with the dark hue overtaking me. I hold my blade up as I ram into her harder and harder. I slash into her soft supple flesh, enjoying the way the knife slices through her.

"Again," he commands, lust glimmering in his eyes.

My knife repeats the motion over and over, until my release explodes from my body. Pulling out of her, I yank the condom from my softening cock and sling it on the table before lifting the dead weight from Tanner.

"She's more beautiful like this," he comments, watching as I drop her to the floor. My body heaves with the beast screaming under my skin. When I let him free, it's an indescribable high that takes hours to come down from.

My body, fully naked and coated in the sticky essence of Dina, puffs and hums before him, the knife tightly gripped in my hand with her blood merging at the tip.

Tanner brings himself to a sitting position, his cock

still hard and present from the opening in his slacks.

Our eyes meet for a long, lust-possessed moment. When the beast is raging, my obsession and focus are dimmed. My body is fueled by a need I don't have control over. It burns on instinct.

"You didn't come," I observe, my voice dark and dripping in a tone I hardly recognize.

"I didn't." His cock jerks at his words, but he makes no moves to touch it.

"She didn't turn you on?" Absently, I rub my palm across my hard chest, enjoying the slickness of Dina's blood coating my flesh.

His amber eyes flicker and darken as he watches my movement. "The sound of her last breath and seeing her blood all over *your* body turns me on." Once again, his cock jolts as his eyes drag over my body.

I'm still trying to figure Tanner out. He's not gay, and he's certainly not straight. I think he's bisexual or something. Definitely somewhere in between. I'm not even sure there's a name for what he is. Tanner has unusual tastes and preferences—like me.

His eyes bore into mine as he lazily takes his thickness in his grip and jerks himself slowly, as if enjoying his visual sexual moment more so than his physical one.

The high of the kill doesn't make my anger riot like it used to. When I'm not searching for the perfect doll and getting disappointed when the prey can't live up to that definition, I find taking a life euphoric.

Killing with Tanner only makes my monster prideful of the effect I have on him.

Friends help one another; masters lure their victims

by whatever means.

I slide my blood smeared hand down to my soft cock, and he watches with interest as I rub the blood over it. My dick wakes back up the moment I rub her crimson remnants along my shaft, hardening immediately.

Leaning forward, Tanner swipes his palm over my lower abs, collecting her blood. The touch makes my spine tingle in an unexpected way. Then, he starts jacking off with her blood in his grip. I match his rhythm and meet his hard glare. I'm not gay or into guys, but Tanner has helped me more than I could ever repay. Recognizing and tuning into what turns him on is something I can do. Not to mention, it only strengthens a bond I need.

Brotherly.

Best friends.

Partners.

Master and Monster. Only…he doesn't know the roles yet.

Leaning back, he pumps himself faster. When his eyes close and he lets out a guttural groan, it speaks to the roaring monster within me. He spurts out his release, and from my standing position, mine showers down, drenching his slacks. I can't help the fierce possessiveness that claws away inside me at the thought of marking him much like an animal would.

He thinks he found me and I'm his little protégé.

But I'm not sure he realizes *I'm* the collector. Like the dolls I made and adored, I find what I like, sculpt and mold it to perfection, then I keep it. I fucking keep it and never let go.

Tanner is my possession.

I'm going to keep him too.

Best friend or brother or goddamned errand runner.

Whichever capacity binds us is the avenue I'll travel to make sure I keep him. And as he reminds me often, I must exercise patience. In order to get what I want, I have to put in the time and make zero mistakes.

Helping Tanner climax by giving in to his unusual desires is just another step in the direction of my plan. I like when he needs me. Even something as simple as being an accomplice in helping him orgasm. His need will fester and grow into something uncontrollable. I'll make sure of it. He's part of my collection—an array of pieces in my life that lead to *my* ultimate happiness.

Because what man *wouldn't* be happy when he has his best friend, his long-lost sister, and his favorite doll all together in one place?

The real world calls this a family.

I call this mine.

CHAPTER FOUR

~ *Modish* ~

Elizabeth

I LIKE BEING WATCHED.
It's a sickness. A perversion. A love for attention.

This affliction isn't something that started at birth or some silly psychological problem passed on by my twisted father. The problem I suffer is solely due to the fact that I'm the lesser *everything* when it comes to my twin sister, Elise, and me.

She excels in her studies. *I fail.*

She draws guys like bees to honey. *They tend not to notice me.*

She's funny, clever, and charismatic. *I'm withdrawn and somber.*

I spend so much of my time watching and wishing I could be like her, but it's all wasted effort. We're not the same. Two girls who shared the same womb for nine months, but we couldn't be more different if we tried.

Physically, we're the same.

Same long dark brown hair. Same slightly upturned nose with a smattering of freckles. The same hazel eyes. Our mouths even smile the same exact way.

But despite that, the guys like her better. She dresses trendy, wears lots of makeup, and has a bubbly personality that makes her laugh a lot.

As for me?

I'm seen as her quiet, strange sister.

I came out of our mother first, yet they treat me as though I'm much younger than her.

She's the light, and I'm the shadow she casts.

So when I do get attention, I bask in it. Like the warm rays of the sun, I want to curl up under it and sleep with it bathing me. The most attentive people in my life are Dillon, Jade, and little MJ. I feel like I belong to their family more than my own. After Dad was found guilty of raping and killing many women, our family was torn apart.

Mom refused to discuss his crimes with us, but it was all over the news, newspapers, internet. She couldn't escape it, and neither could we. She closed her clinic when patients stopped coming to appointments and started working at the hospital. Her hours became long and brutal as she tried to prove herself—to hold everything together financially since she's now putting two kids through college on only her salary. And my sister is busy being Miss Popular College Girl. Our father's black smudge on our lives didn't even leave a mark on her, but people look at me with raised brows and whisper when I pass them.

Hateful comments about my father were slung at me, and questions about a brother I never knew existed. One thing I did learn: pure darkness has its cracks and that's where the light seeps in. It's one of the reasons I'm taking a semester off. I can't stand their judgmental eyes always on me. At least, at home, I'm free from it all.

Being disconnected from your mother and sister makes you question if you're more like the other side of the DNA that created you, and that is a scary prospect.

So, when Dillon and Jade invite me to dinner, I always go. When they need me to watch MJ, I always do. When they simply want to catch up and ask about me, I always chat with them.

The attention I'm feeling right now isn't at all like their warm, sunshiny rays of love. This is different. Like a cool breeze skittering across your damp-with-sweat neck. It sends a chill rippling down your spine.

Dark and sinister.

Frightening.

But still...*someone's* focus.

I always feel eyes on me—unseen and never pinpointed. But they're there all right. And because I like them, even though they feel wrong, I tend to make myself available to those eyes. There are more people like him than I'd ever thought possible.

My bedroom window is open.

The curtains flutter with small gusts of warm wind every so often.

It's dark out there and bright in my room.

I'm in the spotlight. The star of the one-person show.

"Are you sure you don't want to go out tonight?" Elise questions, her brows furrowed together as she studies my appearance.

"Positive." I smile tightly, not missing the way her shoulders relax slightly at my answer. She invites me out of obligation, but revels in the way I always say no.

"Jason's been asking about you," she says as she walks

into the room and stands behind me at my vanity. *Jason?* Gross.

Our eyes meet as she toys with a strand of my hair. Her eyes are rimmed in a smoky black liner and her lashes are painted dark. Elise seems older lately. More exotic. A woman.

My gaze falls to my pale, natural flesh and pouty lips. I'm just a child.

"Jason isn't my type," I tell her, my voice strained with irritation. The last time I gave in and went out with her and her friends, Jason tried to feel me up at the movie theater. His breath reeked of salty butter and he gave me the creeps. Sure, I like attention, but not from an arrogant nerd who thinks he'll nail the shy, desperate girl.

I have standards.

And tastes.

Movie flavored man-boy isn't it.

I prefer something darker, mature, decadent—everything Jason is not.

"Fine," Elise says with a huff. "Mom wants to meet up Saturday for pedicures. She's been working sixteen hour days and crashing at the hospital. That's really the only time we'll get to see her for a while. Don't let her down, okay?"

I'm not the one with a bulging-with-activities calendar.

Although, tonight, I have a couple things on the agenda…

I hate how she tells me Mom's been staying at the hospital, like I wouldn't know. I'm the only occupant of our house and see Mom more than she does. Elise stays on campus. It's just another jab at me. Always jabbing, that perfect twin of mine.

The doorbell rings and Elise jolts away from me, a grin spreading up to her high cheekbones.

"That might be my friend coming to pick me up."

Kami, Elise's newish best friend, is quirky and appears to be more like me than Elise, but with Elise so caught up in herself, I doubt she's even noticed the alternative music Kami likes, or the scattering of thin scars up her forearms from cutting. Elise doesn't see details; not like I do. I like to study people and figure out what keeps their coils moving.

She bounds away, and once again, the stage is all mine. My eyes dart over to the open window and I strain to see outside. No moving figures. Nothing. But I feel those eyes on me. Always. I was sure I was being followed the other day while walking back from a quick shop run. Heavy footfalls sounded behind me, but whenever I would look, the empty stretch of road greeted me.

"Is there anyone out there?" I whisper, scanning the street.

A smile plays at my lips until I hear Elise laughing downstairs. Dillon's deep voice carries up the stairs, and my heart swells in my chest. I wonder if Jade and MJ are with him.

"She never leaves the house," Elise groans, her voice soft as though I can't hear her big mouth anyway.

"Safer that way," Dillon grunts back.

I beam at my reflection in the mirror. I can always count on Dillon to have my back.

"There's nothing to worry about. Maybe she'd have a social life if she ever came with me. But…" she murmurs, her voice is so low I can barely make out what she's saying, "can you please check this out? I know things with our father and the thing he spawned had an effect on her, but this is getting out of hand, and people at my school mentioned this to me, so it's not like she's even hiding it…" her voice trails off into a inaudible whisper, and I'm agitated I can't hear anymore.

My sister huffs when the doorbell rings again, and I can't help but be thankful for the interruption. "Bye, D. My ride is here. Kiss MJ for me."

The front door slams and boots pound up the stairs. Soon, Dillon's giant frame fills my doorway. Paper crumples in his fist and he shoves it into his shirt pocket. He must have come right after work. He's wearing a crisp white button-down shirt that clings to his muscles in a way that makes my heart race. His slacks hug his toned thighs, and I can see the outline of his badge in his pocket.

Are you a cop, or are you just happy to see me?

"What are you smirking about?" he says on a laugh, his shoulder leaning against the frame.

"The very idea that Elise thinks I would go anywhere with Jason Jackoff Bronson," I lie.

His eyebrow arches, but he doesn't call me out on my fib. One of the downsides of having a detective as a friend: he and his wife are way too intuitive. "Is that the fuckwit who got handsy in the theater last time?"

Dillon sees everything about me. He remembers everything about me. This makes him one of my favorite people.

"That's the one. How's Jade? I felt the baby move last time she was here," I tell him, spinning in my desk chair, a small smile tugging at my lips.

He grins and walks through my room to the window. My heart rate quickens. What if he scares those eyes away? I nearly sigh aloud when he closes the window and turns the lock. Drawing the curtains together, he turns to me.

"She's fine." His brows furrow, and I can tell something is bothering him. I notice things too.

"What's wrong?"

"You shouldn't leave windows open, especially when you're alone in the house."

I quirk a brow. "I'm not alone. You're here," I tease. "What's really wrong?"

His jaw clenches and hands ball into fists. "I saw some pretty gruesome shit yesterday. It worries the fuck out of me that something will happen to you or Elise. Your mom is never home and you guys are out here all alone." He scrubs at his scruffy cheek with his palm. "Especially you."

We've grown real close since Dad's incarceration, and it makes you realize family isn't always who you share your blood with. It's the ones who take care of you, love you, and stay around.

"I'm nineteen," I remind him, picking up a pen and doodling on the pad that holds so many secrets.

He gives me a clipped nod, but a storm brews in his eyes. It makes me uncomfortable the way he surveys everything in my bedroom. When his gaze falls to my closet, I cringe.

"You'd tell me if something was wrong, right, nugget?" His eyebrow lifts in question as he saunters over to the closet. "Like if you were doing the marijuana."

I snort with a laugh and roll my eyes. Sometimes he

reminds me of my father, but I would never burden him with that non-compliment. "You're a dork. I'm not *doing the marijuana*. And yes, I'd tell you if something were wrong."

But right now, most everything is right.

By the way his eyes keep darting over to the closet, curiosity shining in them and his gaze lingering, I can tell he really wants to peek inside, but I don't give him the permission he desperately wants. "Want to stay for dinner? I could reheat the pork chops and mashed potatoes I made earlier."

His stomach grumbles, and I laugh.

"As much as I'd love to take you up on that offer, I promised Jade I'd swing by to check on you and get my big ass home. Apparently, MJ has been giving her fits if I'm not there to read her a bedtime story." Abandoning his curiosity of my closet, he walks over to me, and I stand to hug him. His fingers brush down to the scribbles on the pad cover, and my body hums and trembles as if the ground quakes beneath me. Swallowing, I will myself to relax.

"Maybe Sunday, if you guys are free, come over and you can teach me how to use the grill again. Last time, I almost burned down the house, but I'm dying for home-cooked burgers on the grill."

He regards me with affection. In his eyes, I'm like a little sister to him. And unlike being in Elise's shadow, being in Dillon's shadow is different. He craves to protect me, teach me, and mold me since I don't have many people in my life who can do that for me, and I crave his affection, approval, comfort.

"Of course, nugget."

I follow him downstairs, hugging him once more, and inhale his mix of sweat and aftershave. As he saunters off to his vehicle, I wave to him. The feeling of being watched seems to intensify, the hairs on the back of my neck raising in awareness. Dillon drives away, and my gaze sweeps across the darkness, searching for those eyes.

Finding nothing, I deflate a little, and close the door, twisting the lock into place. I make sure to do the same in my bedroom. Not that I'm afraid of anyone. Now that I'm alone, I'm free to be me.

My hand hovers over the notebook left so carelessly for anyone to snoop within. I flick my fingers through the pad, opening to the page with big scribbled letters.

BENNY

The picture the media used while trying to hunt him down and one with our dad when he was small are the only ones they had. The artist's rendering of him is spooky. Something about the dark, vacant eyes. Sometimes, I stare at the picture, willing it to come to life just so I can ask my brother some questions. News clippings are also stuck to the pages, and my heart slows as I turn the page and stare down at flames I'd hand drawn around a tombstone, remembering the day I learned of Benjamin when Elise educated me on his demise.

Nearly three years ago...

Elise still goes to classes and acts like life is normal when in the cold reality, life—ours, at least—is anything but. Eyes follow me as I cross the courtyard and drop my bag under the giant tree offering shelter from the overbearing heat. My skin protests the sun—literally. It gets red and angry when exposed. My pale complexion has always been something I've liked about myself...until I started junior high and boys made fun of me.

Vampire.

Milk bottle.

And the more cultured students went with Geisha girl, like that was an insult. Skin paling is a billion-dollar industry in Asia.

I'm brought from my musing when a girl I know as Fakebitch One sits down next to me. Her friends, Fakebitch Two and Three, stand beside her like her personal bodyguards.

I hold my hand over my eyes to block the sun and look over her perfect features. Blue eyes, blonde hair curling around her pretty oval shaped face, a plump bottom lip with a thin top lip. She smirks, then speaks, handing me an iPad I hadn't realized she was carrying.

"So, do you know where your brother is? Like, did he sneak you messages to let you know he's okay?"

Oh God, she thinks I'm someone else. My mouth parts, but words don't form.

Lifting her hand, she waves it in front of my face. "Hello, earth to..." she looks up at her friend, who scrunches her shoulders and mouths, "Beck?"

"...Beck," she mimics, turning back to face me.

My glower goes unnoticed as she stares back at me. "It's Beth. Elizabeth," I retort.

"Whatever." She rolls her eyes and taps at the screen

now in my lap.

My eyes drop to the page she's brought up.

Killer Chief of Police, Steve Stanton, covers up heinous crimes of son who is still at large. Now labeled THE DOLL KILLER by the press, Benjamin Stanton is being hunted by police for the murders of numerous women and abduction and imprisonment of a female detective.

Here is what we know…

Benjamin is the only son of the shamed rapist and murderer, Steve Stanton, conceived by his first wife, Patricia Stanton. She is believed to be one of the victims whose remains were amongst those recovered from a property belonging to Steve Stanton. A doll maker by trade, Patricia molded her son's fascination and ultimate obsession with porcelain dolls.

Before I can read more, the IPad is snatched from my grasp and Fakebitch One is grinning at me. "So…does he reach out?"

Is she serious?

"Why?"

She shrugs her shoulders, and her friends giggle. "It's just kind of hot."

"This isn't true." I shake my head. "I don't have a brother."

"This is a legit source, Becka. She blogs online, but her source is someone on the inside."

"It's Beth, and I don't care who her source is."

"She says he dressed up his victims and fucked them, and if they weren't good, he killed them."

More giggles sound from her friends.

"I think I could be a great doll," she coos.

She's insane.

"*So, you want to be raped and murdered?*"

If what she's saying is true, that's what she wants to happen to her?

"*He wouldn't kill me, silly. I'd be the perfect doll for him.*"

"*He might be gross looking,*" *one of her friends pipes in.*

Tossing her hair over her shoulder, Fakebitch One glowers up at her outspoken friend and humphs. "*I told you, Kate. I saw the leaked sketch before it was taken down and he's super hot.*"

"*Oh, yeah, I forgot,*" *her friend backpedals.*

"*None of this is relevant,*" *I grit out.* "*I don't have a brother. One killer in the family is enough. Thank you, though. If I ever do run across him, I'll be sure to send him to your address.*"

I stand, grabbing my backpack, and get roughly ten feet before she calls out, "*Do you know my address?*"

Idiot.

My palms sweat and my heart paces. I need to find Elise. I need to call Jade or Dillon—or both.

I locate Elise in the girl's bathroom smacking her newly applied lipstick and brushing through her hair.

"*Wendy Hudson just spoke to me,*" *I spit out.*

Lowering her brush, Elise's eyes clash with mine in the mirror.

"*Did she think you were me?*" *she asks, her eyes raking over my attire.*

"*No. She wanted information on our brother.*"

Elise's face pales and she spins to face me.

Oh my God. It's true.

"What did she say?"

"What does that matter? How come you don't look surprised at the mention of a freaking brother?"

She covers my mouth with her hand and looks around the empty bathroom.

"Mom mentioned it by accident, and I called her on it. She confessed our father had a family before us."

"A family, or a son?" My stomach twists and stirs.

"Just a son, I think." She shrugs her shoulders like she's talking about the weather or something of less importance.

"And he is a murderer too?" I whisper, wrapping my arms around my waist.

"Mom said he was messed up by two deranged parents, that his mental state would have been fragmented from a young age. He's a product of his environment."

Oh my God.

Confusion within my emotions battles for space inside my head.

I have a brother?

No, you have another killer.

A damaged brother?

No, a deranged murderer.

Was he left alone all this time?

Or did he want to be left alone to kill?

Did our father abandon him?

To raise us?

What was his mother like?

What if she was our mother too, would we be like him?

Why did he become this…this killer?

"And he's out there?" I question.

Her hands come down on my shoulders, a stoic look on her face.

"No, don't be frightened. This can't go any further, Beth,"

Instead of responding, I wait for her to continue.

"Dillon told Mom to stop her worrying about him being out there. He's dead. Died in a fire, but it wasn't reported, so only a few people know."

My feet begin moving despite her calling out my name.

"Beth…Beth?"

I pass Wendy in the corridor and turn back to grab her arm. Her mouth pops open and she whines as I drag her over to the lockers.

Scanning the halls, she hush whispers, "Just because I spoke to you outside, it doesn't mean you can approach me in the halls."

Seriously?

"I want to know the name of the person who runs that blog."

Her arms fold over her perfectly formed breasts, pushing them farther out from the V-neck of her cashmere sweater. Smirking, she tosses her hair over her shoulder and jerks her chin.

"So, it is true?"

"Wendy," *I hiss.*

"It's an anonymous blog so she can't be targeted or chastised for what she writes."

"Name?"

"What makes you think I know it?"

"Wendy."

"You can have her email, but she may not reply."

Digging into my backpack, I hand her a pad and pen. Smacking her lips together with a tutting sound, she scribbles the address down and saunters off without a glance back.

"Beth," Elise whisper-yells at me from a doorway leading to English.

"What?"

"What are you doing? We have class."

"I don't." *I push through the doors to the yard and make my way home to email this blogger.*

My hand grasps the email I received back from the anonymous blogger almost three years ago. A case file from a profiler created on Benjamin before they knew who he was.

A loner, possibly from a one-parent family with anger toward both.

Abandonment issues. A longing to be accepted and loved. Knows what he does is wrong, but the impulsion is rooted too deep, possibly due to an abusive parent.

They weren't far off. I think about how troubled he was. His actions of taking lives was unacceptable, but that's all he knew growing up. His parents did the same thing and didn't hide it. Instead, they shared the insanity like it was normalcy. Would any of us turn out this way? Or was the sickness something he was born with from bad DNA? Nature versus nurture…we'll never know.

My life changed that day. I changed and found myself.

Pulling my curtains open, I slide my window back up. The temperature has cooled some, eliciting a shiver.

I always feel eyes on me. Always. I hug my robe tighter around me as I make my way to my closet. Once I open it, I stare at my tall armoire inside. It keeps my secrets locked in it—secrets that might cause friction if Dillon or Elise were to find out.

With a gasp of excitement, I retrieve my key from my robe pocket, unlock the armoire, and pull open the two mahogany doors. Around my family and friends, I may dress simple and boring, but when I'm alone, I enjoy wearing pretty dresses. I love frills and lace. I love how easy it is to become someone else.

I choose the white dress that reminds me of when Elise and I were five and Mom dressed us up to sit on the Easter Bunny's lap. Elise screamed in horror, but I loved the big, animated bunny. I snuggled against his faux fur, adoring the way he hugged me to him.

Untying the sash on my robe, I let it fall to my feet in a heap. My bra is simple and white. The panties I'm wearing I made myself, stitching lacy ruffles on the bottom. They're quite adorable. I want everyone to see them, especially the imaginary eyes outside. Ever since I can remember, I've loved to create my own style, which led to making my own clothes.

My heart hammers in my chest as I pull the white dress from the hanger and tug it on over my head. It falls into place. Modest in the chest area, not showing too much, but short enough to feel girly and slightly sexy in an innocent way. I pull open one of the drawers and hunt for some white knee-highs. Once I slip those on over my long legs, I admire how the material hugs my flesh. My skin is pale, but the knee-highs are paler. Locating my shiny black Mary Janes, I slip them on, then twist my long, dark locks into a bun and pin it into place. My favorite wig hangs alongside my handmade dresses, and I finger the silky red piece before slipping it on over my hair. Once I tug it into place, I'm ready for some makeup.

My gaze is drawn to the window once more. Someone is out there. I can practically feel their eyes licking over the soft planes of my body. The heat from it prickles my skin in a way that doesn't quite burn, but teases instead. Sometimes, I wish whoever was out there would show their face, creep through the window, and show me I'm not as alone as I feel.

The ghost of a man I never knew haunts me.

I spend a good half hour applying my makeup, highlighting my youth while focusing on my pouty lips. The false lashes are always the trickiest, but eventually, I get them glued into place. Batting them like the wings of a butterfly, they fan over the rose apples of my cheeks. When I glance at my reflection, a shy smile tugs at my lips.

Almost ready.

Pulling out my laptop, I set it on my vanity once I've cleared away the makeup. It takes a few minutes to log in, but I finally get where I want to be. Where I'm the star of my show. Where thousands of people wait for this moment—a moment with me.

I attempt to still my racing heart, but I can't. The anticipation thrumming through me is what keeps me alive. This life is too hollow and dull and sad without these moments. They fulfil a part of me that's needed filling since the moment our father was sent to jail. Everyone tried their best to keep us out of the spotlight, and they succeeded. But what they couldn't do was keep me from watching it all over the news. What my father did. What my half-brother did. All the horrors. The strange fetishes. The captives. The murders. My father went to prison, and my half-brother was burned alive, according to Dillon. He died, and all the bad things were supposed to die with him.

But some things were born after his death.

Some things were carried on.

I push the button that thrusts me into my world. Tonight is going to be different. I won't sit in silence or just take pictures for my observers to view.

"Hello," I squeak, my voice soft and childlike. "Who wants to sing me a bedtime song?" I pout my lips as I watch hundreds of user names comment, so fast, I can't read them. "Nobody," I lie, chewing on my bottom lip. "I suppose I'll have to sing one to myself then."

My private message box lights up and I watch the number quadruple within seconds. Sometimes, when I feel like no one sees me, I go in and read all the adoring messages. Some are dirty and perverted. Others are sweet and fatherly. Each and every one promises to take care of me.

"Miss Polly had a dolly who was sick, sick, sick,
So she phoned for the doctor to be quick, quick, quick.
The doctor came with his bag and his hat,
And he knocked at the door with a rat-a-tat-tat.
He looked at the dolly and he shook his head,
And he said, "Miss Polly, put her straight to bed!"
He wrote on a paper for a pill, pill, pill,
"I'll be back in the morning, yes I will, will, will."

CHAPTER FIVE

~ Latest ~

Benny

I STARE AT THE SCREEN in wonder. Tanner has gone off to do God knows what, saying he'd be back with dinner, so I'm taking the moment to watch *her*.

Pretty new doll.

The urge to go see my Bethany was overwhelming, but when Tanner is giving you his attention, you don't blow him off for your own needs. After we fucked and killed Dina, we drank whiskey and talked about my plans for procuring my sister. Stalking her and whacking off in my car wasn't on the agenda—at least, not for tonight.

So, even though I don't have time to see her, I do have time to visit my newest fascination. Pretty New Doll. Pulling up the website, I was elated to discover she's doing a live feed.

I watch her fat lips, swollen and perfect. She's not looking directly into the camera, and I want to reach through the screen and tilt her chin. So perfect. Pale skin that's such a contrast to the pink of her lips and tint to her cheeks. The red abomination on her head looks wiry; certainly not her own. It must go. Her lips part as they murmur words that still my breath.

My heart beat.

My soul.

Her voice sings to parts of my dark soul I didn't know wanted to be sung to. She takes awful memories of my mother and turns them into something soothing. Her sweetly sung words wash over me like a warm summer rain.

This can't be real. That song. Her. My eyes focus on her lips, and my chest heaves with heavy pants.

This pretty new doll could suck on my cock for hours and I'd never grow tired of watching the way her plump lips turn red from rubbing up and down my length.

She could sit on my lap and sing to me while I dropped my fingers between the fabric of the cotton panties I'd insist she wear.

After a hot shower earlier, I wrapped my waist in a towel. Now, as I watch this new doll on the screen, my dick aches for attention. It's jerking and throbbing and fucking angry, peeking out from the edge of the towel like a python in the bushes waiting to pounce—to fucking devour.

Pretty New Doll mentions something about being a good girl for the doctor and having to go to bed, and my breath gets sucked from my chest as she climbs onto her bed with her back to the screen. Her long red hair hangs down her back in waves, nearly touching her ass. When she starts crawling across the bed toward her pillows, I'm awarded the view of a sliver of creamy flesh between the hem of her dress and knee-highs.

"I wonder when the doctor will come make me all better," she ponders aloud. Bending forward to reach for her pillows, she plumps them, and her dress lifts enough to show her white lacy panties.

Thud.
Thud.
Thud.

"Fuck me," I growl.

My cock gets yanked into my fist and I jerk hard on it. She's such a perfect doll. Her outfit. Her face. Her fucking everything. I want to rip her red hair from her skull—it's the only thing not right on her—but all that can be changed once Tanner finds her for me. He blabbed on about his hacker Luke and IP addresses, which meant nothing to me. All I heard was a promise. A motherfucking vow. And if Tanner is good at anything, it's keeping his word.

He *better* keep it.

I don't tear my gaze from her sexy ass as I fuck my hand. It won't be long before I'm inside her. I'll get to hear the way she begs and pleads and fucking sings. How my name moaned on her lips will sound. I'll get to defile her and steal her innocence.

A knock pounds on her bedroom door, and she shrieks.

"I forgot my wallet," a woman's voice hollers through the door. "Elizabeth, did I leave it in there?"

Elizabeth.

Pretty New Doll's eyes fly to the computer screen, and I take a good look at her familiar eyes beneath the fake lashes for the first time. The terror and guilt of being caught shines in their gorgeous hazel depths, which are no doubt perfect. I come abruptly, the heat scorching my chest as it spurts out suddenly.

"Elizabeth!" the woman yells again.

"It's not here," Pretty New Doll bites back, her voice no longer childlike. It's familiar. I've heard it before, and that face…those eyes.

Bethany.

No.

Yes.

She doesn't say anything more, but rushes toward the screen. My heart stutters and attacks the cage confining it. Her hand reaches forward, shutting down the feed immediately.

I close my eyes and replay her voice over and over again to be sure, but I know I am. I knew there was a reason I was so drawn to this new doll.

Bethany.

Bethany.

Bethany.

She called her Elizabeth. Elizabeth is my Bethany.

Fuck.

"Here," Tanner murmurs, tossing me a rag to clean myself up with.

I jerk my head his way, a little shocked to see him. I'd been so wrapped up in what I was doing, I never heard him come in.

"It's her," I spit out as I wipe away the cum on my chest and stand. His gaze falls to my flaccid cock, and his lips twitch. I never know what's going on beyond his amber eyes.

He tugs at his tie a little and pierces me with a bored stare. "I know."

Snatching up my jeans from the floor, I yank them up my thighs. Once I've fastened them, I fold my bulky arms over my tattooed chest and glare. "What the fuck do you mean, you know?"

Is he playing games?

Does he think I'm a slave to his mind fucks?

His hard gaze softens and he frowns as he sits on the edge of my bed. "I've known all along. It's not hard to find someone's IP address. I've known her location from the moment I first saw her."

Betrayal cuts through my chest like a knife. My jaw clenches and nostrils flare. "This better be good, Tanner. Go on."

His jaw tightens, and a simmering rage that always lurks inside him flickers in his eyes.

"I discovered it was her—your *Bethany*. I knew Stanton very well, Benjamin, so I knew he had a wife." He lets out a frustrated sigh. The fact that he's not as put together as normal has me wondering what the hell is going on with him.

"Why didn't you tell me, goddammit?" I seethe.

He stands back up, and with it, his authority wraps around him like a cloak, the single moment of vulnerability gone.

"You need to remember who you're speaking to," he snaps, his chest heaving. "I didn't tell you because you lose your fucking mind over your dolls and your past. Plus, I wanted to be sure. I wanted to help line this out for you. To motherfucking *surprise* you, asshole." His lips quirk up on one side. "Surprise."

I'm not amused with his coy games tonight. "You let

me watch her. I need her. I need to go get her right now." I point to the black screen. "Don't you see? She's done this for me. It's fucking fate. Bethany knows I love dolls—that I love her. She's become the perfect doll for me. For. Me. This is her call for help. Bethany wants me to find her and bring her home. She sang the song."

Tanner's eyes darken. "She thinks you're dead, Monster."

Cold reality splashes over me and I gape at him. "Then who does she do this for?"

He shrugs. "For them, I suppose, but it would appear she may be honoring your memory in her own way."

"Fuck that," I roar. "She's doing it for *me*. How do you know what she thinks? For all we know, she's holding out hope I'm still alive. Why would she assume otherwise?"

"Not what Kami says. They know you died in a fire." His tone is matter of fact.

I take a threatening step toward him, my hand fisting at my side. "Who in the fuck is Kami? The girl who called out to her on the feed?"

Something flashes in his eyes, and I lock away that look to ponder later—when I'm not flipping my shit over finding Bethany.

"No, she's an associate of mine. I hired her to befriend Elise. Collect intel." He steps closer, regarding me with an impish grin. "All for you, Monster. You know you're my favorite."

"Who is Elise?"

He's in the middle of pouring himself a whiskey and raises the glass, letting out a snort. "Oh, Benjamin," he says, as if I should know all this shit. "Elise is Elizabeth's, *your Bethany's*, twin sister."

My mouth drops open, then closes as thoughts of there being two of them out there send my mind into chaos.

"Don't get too excited, Monster. They're polar opposites. Elise wouldn't last long under your command."

"I want Bethany," I snarl.

He clutches my shoulder. "I know you do. Soon. I promise."

The tightness in my chest doesn't let up, but I do relax some. "Fine. My cells aren't ready anyway, but I want to talk to this Kami person. I *need* to talk to her."

His eyes narrow, as if he has the ability to peer inside my brain. "That can be arranged."

"Now," I clarify. "Give me her address. I'll pay her a visit."

"Fine," he grits out. "But you won't need to go that far. She lives at the club. Let's go."

I follow Tanner down a long corridor inside The Vault, confused by what he meant when he said she lives here. The walls vibrate with music, but it's quieter in the back, and it's then I realize I've never been to this part of the premises before. He takes me into what seems like just an office, but it's so much more.

A massive desk dominates the head of the room, overlooking a huge square see-through box. Inside is a bed made of transparent plastic. A toilet sits in one corner, but nothing more. There's a latch hole integrated into the door of the box, and all around are cameras pointing to it. My eyes scan the rest of the room, landing on a small leather couch to the right where a tiny blonde with silky, pink-streaked hair sits on her cell. Her lip is caught between her teeth as she texts, ignoring the two tyrants who just walked in the room. I want to rip the phone from her hand and demand answers, but Tanner is back in "I'm the motherfucking master of the universe" mode, so I hang back.

For now.

"Kami." His greeting is low and filled with authority.

She drags her gaze from the small screen and shoots him a slow, private smile, as if I'm not standing here on motherfucking pins and needles waiting for answers. I grunt, hoping Tanner gets my drift to move things along.

"Anything new with Elise?"

"Besides the fact that she's drunk and making out with some guy old enough to be her dad on the dance floor at Vogue right now? Nope, nothing new," she says with an unamused huff. "She will be going home with him, so I took that as my cue to leave." A giggle escapes her.

Her goddamn laugh is like nails on a chalkboard. This bitch is getting on my fucking nerves and it's taking everything in me not to go off on her—not to grab her by her skinny throat and slam her against the bookshelf behind her.

"I need to know everything you know about Bethany," I snap, my fury rippling through me.

Her nose scrunches in confusion. "Who's Bethany?"

White hot anger surges through me.

"Elizabeth," Tanner clarifies, holding a hand to my chest to stop me advancing forward, his voice easy and placating. I hate that he's being so fucking nice and tolerant with her. Who the hell is she and why has he never mentioned a woman living here?

"What do you want to know?"

"Everything," I snarl.

She stands and shoves her phone in her pocket. "Shy. A bit on the nerdy side. Elise thinks she's hiding some dark secret but won't tell me what. Obviously, I know Elizabeth is on a fetish website, but Elise doesn't know I know. Not much to tell. She hates this guy Jason. Apparently Elise keeps trying to set them up, but Elizabeth keeps shooting her down."

"She's mine," I hiss as I stalk over to her.

The bitch doesn't flinch, which pisses me off. Iron balls, this one. I want to rip them from her—show her why she needs to fear people like me.

"Whatever, man. I'm just there for the gossip to bring home to Boss Man." She shrugs. "That's all."

That.

Is.

Not.

All.

"I need to know *everything*," I repeat, my voice low and deadly. "I need you to stop giving me this watered-down version and tell me every single thing about her."

"That's all," she challenges.

This bitch…

Snatching her by her tiny throat, I squeeze the fuck out of her. I'm about to slam her into the shelves behind her when her arm comes up and over, slicing down across my arm with exceptional power, forcing my arm to drop. I'm so shocked by this turn of events, I don't prepare for her shoving me backwards with two hands against my shoulders and following it up with a thrust of her leg, her knee colliding with my gut, robbing me of breath.

Motherfucker.

A fighter.

This will be fun.

I spit the acid she forced up my throat to the floor and prowl toward her. A smile graces her lips, highlighting what a beautiful face she has—*had*, by the time I'm finished with her. Before I get close, Tanner yanks me hard, and I stumble, my equilibrium thrown off balance. He shoves me to the ground hard with little effort and tackles me like a fucking psycho.

Tanner is always poised, amused, and chill. Sometimes, darkness lurks, but I don't ever see him lose his shit. Ever. The rage blazing in his eyes is shocking.

"Don't. Touch. My. Associate." His fists yank at my shirt as he spits out his words. "Understand, *friend*?" The fat vein in his neck pulsates with each ragged breath he takes.

"I understand, *friend*," I bite back, my own anger still very much at the surface. "Now, get the fuck off me."

What the actual fuck?

Since when has he ever put a leash on me?

Called someone off limits?

My thoughts discombobulate, and I struggle to find even ground once more. The red bleeds from his flesh some, and a smile tugs at his lips. He playfully slaps my cheek before standing and offering his hand. Once I'm back on my feet, I glare at Kami. This girl has got to go. Tanner is protective over her, and I don't like it. He caged me in front of her, showed power over me, showed favor to her.

Tanner protects *me*.

And *he's* mine.

My own personal master doll reaping with the hand of death.

The dumb blonde with the pink in her hair is merely a distraction—a wrench in my plans. I've worked hard to become Tanner's favorite thing. I don't need anyone knocking me off my pedestal.

And because I play a better game than the pair of tits in the room, I stand close enough to Tanner's back that my body heat mixes with his, rest my forehead on his shoulder, and let out a pained sigh.

"I just *need* her," I explain, my words meant only for him.

His stiff posture relaxes, and I'm elated by how easily I'm able to work myself inside Tanner. It makes my cock hard. With a small thrust of my hips, I press my erection against him, reminding him *we're* still the team. Not this bitch. Tanner and I. Master and Monster. *Let me kill her for you*, I convey in my actions.

"Kami," he says, his voice strained. "Don't be coy. We need details. All of them."

I look over his shoulder at her, and her nostrils flare. So, the bitch was trying to piss me off on purpose. Perhaps she likes Tanner in a way he'll never be able to fully reciprocate. I play her like I play him.

"If I'm getting in the way of you sucking his dick,

then by all means, suck away," I say in a cool tone, insinuating she's a whore. "But this shit is important and I need answers." My own cock is still hard, especially when I imagine him ramming his dick down her throat until she suffocates. I shamelessly press against Tanner's ass while maintaining the bitch's stare. The challenge flickering in her blue eyes is all I need to know about her.

She wants him so fucking bad.

Get in line, cunt. He's mine, and I don't even have to fuck him.

"Actually," Tanner growls as he steps away from me. "Why don't you suck off my dear friend here? He's the one with the aching hard-on."

Fuck.

Sometimes I forget how perceptive Tanner is. Beating him at his own game is difficult—especially when he knows he's being played. His suggestion for her to suck my dick is a test. Always tests with this guy.

And he's testing her too.

Pain furrows her brow, her eyes lowering and hands clenching. "I'm no one's whore, Cassian," she says in a bored tone, the lie as fake as her tits. She would be a whore for him. The fact she calls him by another name—the same name Lucy uses—isn't news, but I store it away anyway to revisit later. "But I'd be more than happy to talk about Elizabeth."

Rolling my eyes, I sit down on the leather sofa. "Well, since I'm not getting my dick sucked by *you* tonight, please do continue," I mutter. "Maybe later I can find *someone* to put their lips on my cock."

This time, the challenge is for Tanner, and to plant

the seed in this girl's head that her precious "boss man" does it to me. Drop the seeds, watch them grow, and cause chaos.

The motherfucker just laughs.

"Storytime, Kami." He sits down beside me and relaxes. "And make it a good one."

CHAPTER SIX

~ *Distinct* ~

Elizabeth

Banging on the front door rouses me from slumber. I jackknife up in my bed and listen, trying to decipher whether it was real or in my dream.

Bang.
Bang.
Bang.

My heart races as I grab my cell and bring Dillon's contact up, hovering my thumb over the call button. *Could be anything. Don't be paranoid.*

Taking tentative steps down the stairs, every shadow stalks me and each squeak of the floorboard turns my nervous stomach.

"Who's there?" I croak out, but get no answer. Placing the cell down on the side table, I flick the lamp on and grab one of the umbrellas with a metal pick on the end from the basket next to the front door. It will hurt if I ram it hard enough.

I spy through the peephole, but only see a distorted, weirdly portioned street.

Unlatching the door, I swing it open, the umbrella

raised, ready to beat the tormenter with a waterproof stick covered in pink flowers. Elise always had to have everything pink and flowery. Can you imagine if I had to really use it?

"How did he die?"

"A pink flowery umbrella to the chest."

I'm laughing in my head at my over-the-top paranoia, the empty, dark night the only thing greeting me. Must have been the wind.

"What are you doing?"

A scream escapes, and I turn, whacking the stick at a messy looking Elise.

"What the hell?" she screeches, my chest heaving in shock. I think I just knocked ten years off my life expectancy.

"What are you doing here?" I bark as the wind pushes through the open doorway, blowing my hair into my face.

When my breathing gets under control, I take in her appearance. Her hair is disheveled and sticking up all over her head, and her skin is puffy and red beneath the black streaks marring her cheeks.

"I had to break things off with my boyfriend." She sniffles, rubbing her arm where I struck her.

"Boyfriend?"

Shaking her head, she walks to the couch and throws herself on to the cushions.

"It's a long story and everything is a mess."

I frown. "You want to talk about it?"

"Why? So you can gloat that I'm not the perfect person you think I am?" she spits, narrowing her eyes at me.

"No one is perfect, Elise," I inform her.

She huffs. "Well, you certainly aren't."

Crossing my arms over my chest, I glare at her. "What does that mean?"

She lets out a laugh that has no humor attached.

"Oh, come on, Beth," she sneers, a slight wobble to her voice that has me wondering if she's been drinking. "What the hell were you doing earlier? Were you wearing those clothes again? Do you know how messed up your obsession is?" My blood chills because on more than one occasion, my sister has burst through my door and seen me in my fancy outfits and makeup. It's private and I hate that she knows.

"It's *not* an obsession," I hiss. "It's a way to feel connected to *him*. To life. To feeling more than the void inside my chest. Life's always been easy for *you*, but not everyone has the experiences you do."

She stands and shakes her head. "So it's my fault I'm not a depressed freak like you?"

"Tell me how you really feel," I sneer, "you self-righteous bitch."

Her eyes roam behind me and she pales. "What the hell is that?" She points to the still open doorway, and I turn, following her gaze. A package sits in the doorway, wrapped in brown paper. I narrow my eyes, trying to make out the words emblazoned on the front.

Pretty doll for a pretty doll…

Marching over to the package, I retrieve it, slam the door, lock the latch into place, and run up to my room.

"Elizabeth, what the hell is that?" Elise shouts, but I've had enough of her for one night.

I unwrap the paper, excitement and fear battling for control within me. A porcelain doll stares up at me. Perfect detail. Hair curled with a small bonnet sitting on top. The craftsmanship in the clothes is exceptional. My eyes shift back to the box, searching for a note. I don't find one, but still feel compelled to thank the gift supplier even though they came to my house. Fear isn't the victor here—appreciation overrules me.

Someone notices me.

Someone is paying *attention*.

I decide to get my dress on and paint my face to perfection before turning on the camera. My smile is wide and appreciative.

"I want to thank whoever you are for my beautiful gift." I bat my lashes in a flirty way. "The doll now has a dolly of her very own, and she's perfect." I blow a kiss at the screen and log off.

I'm still flying high on adrenaline as I scrub the makeup from my face. Once I'm clean, I pick up the doll from the bed, swipe all the picture frames from one of my shelves into the bin, and put her front and center. Crawling back into bed, I stare at her watching me until I drift into dreams of a man I never got to meet.

A pounding on my bedroom door is relentless. "Fuck off!" I shout, throwing a pillow at it.

"Come on, Beth," Elise whines. "Don't be mad. I'm sorry for what I said last night. I was drunk and sad."

Oh God, I don't care. I just want to sleep in.

"Can we go for coffee? I'll even go to the one in the

bookstore you love so much. My treat. Any title of your choosing."

Sitting up, I rub sleep from my eyes. "Any title?"

She laughs. "Yes, as long as it's under twenty-two dollars and fifty cents."

After an eye-roll, I drag myself from the bed and toss some clothes on. Pulling open the door, I find Elise standing there without a strand of hair out of place. It now has blonde streaks through it, opposite of how she looked last night. There's not one red blip on her skin. Does she use magic cream or what?

"When did you do that to your hair?"

"I went to the salon this morning," she tells me as she bites her bottom lip. "I needed a change."

This morning? What the hell? "What time is it?"

"Nearly noon, lazy. Let's go before it's dinner time."

The smell of coffee overpowers the smell of the paper, but the real appeal is the old secondhand books the store stocks. I love the worn pages, showing how many people have loved and lived the story. Before I found solace in becoming a beautiful doll for my viewers, reading was my escape. Leaving Elise to order drinks, I make my way through the aisles, brushing my fingers over the spines and smiling to myself. I want to build a nook within the bookcases and live here for a while.

Time drifts away from me as I scan the pages of an old Jane Austen novel. My stomach growls, and I realize how long I've left Elise. As I make my way through the stacks, a tall man comes into view. His back is to me as he spies through a gap in a shelf at someone on the opposite side. Butterflies flutter in my stomach. The thought of being watched does things to me, even when I'm not the interest of the voyeur. I silently come up behind him, and his scent invades my space. My head feels woozy from its power—sweat mixed with citrus undertones and something else…soap, the kind you get in hospitals. Maybe he's a surgeon? His body heat permeates from him like a force field. I follow the direction of his head and swallow the bitter laugh I want to choke on. Of course it's Elise he's looking at.

"She just had her heart broken, so go gentle on her," I jest, startling him. He turns to face me, and his eyes widen as his mouth drops open. He has the most intense brown eyes I've ever seen. Pained. Wounded. Sad. All those emotions flicker away in an instant as interest takes over. It has heat flooding through me. Something about him is familiar. I wonder if maybe he's a surgeon where Mom works. I've definitely seen him before. The structure of his face is carved to perfection—an endearing scattering of faint freckles over his nose. A dark brown beard covers his cheeks, accentuating his full pink lips. His shaved head shows tattoos down his neck disappearing inside his shirt. My mouth waters as my eyes move to his chest, wondering if he's covered in tattoos there as well.

"Hi," I say, lifting my hand awkwardly. "She's my sister."

He just stares at me without a single word escaping his lips. So, maybe he's a weirdo. A beautiful, book-loving, delicious smelling weirdo.

"Right. Okay." I blush and turn on my heel to leave,

but he reaches for me. There's something sharp in his hands and it cuts my finger when his hand clasps onto mine. "Ouch." I recoil, and he drops his hand. My eyes dart to the offending item. It's his keys—there's a spiky key ring coated with a small spot of my blood.

"I'm sorry," he grits out, his voice deep and haunted.

My heart flutters dutifully in my chest, reminding me I'm a woman and he's a man. A stunning, broad, tall man.

Reaching out, he takes my hand, and the warmth of his touch has me mesmerized. I watch with pure fascination and awe as he brings my finger to his lips and kisses the small cut, opening his mouth slightly to suck. His tongue is rough on the underside of my finger and my mind flits with dirty images of feeling that tongue in other places…softer places. I'm solidified to the floor, unable to move. He lowers my hand and flashes me a sexy smile. "There. All better."

"Um…thank you?" I murmur.

"You're beautiful," he breathes.

My senses come back to me, jerking my body into waking up from its lust-filled slumber. "Says the man creeping on my sister from the shadows," I tease.

His face screws up in distaste. "No," he snaps in a firm tone. "She's not right. Her presence, the blonde, her attitude, it's all…wrong." His smile is back, his brown eyes twinkling in delight. "But you? You are perfect."

I'm forming three Os with my eyes and mouth, but I can't speak.

"I'll be seeing you," he states simply. A vow—not a question.

My head swims as he passes me and heads to the exit.

Rushing toward Elise, I stumble, letting out a squeak of a scream when a body collides with my own. I gasp in shock at the fleeting pain when hot liquid seeps into my dress on my chest. My eyes drag up the body of a sexy blonde who's wrinkling her nose up at the mess she's caused. Her cleavage bounces from the gaping slit in her top as she mutters a brief, "Sorry." I stare after her as she hightails it for the exit.

Thanks, clumsy Barbie bitch. "You ruined my dress," I call out to her even though she can't hear me.

Several pairs of eyes flicker over me in silent judgment as they take in my now soiled dress. Brown forever will stain the perfect fabric. I ignore their stares because it wasn't my fault.

Frustrated, I storm over to my sister. "Did you see that?" I hiss, swiping at my front as if it will magically disappear. "We need to leave." I hand her my small pile of books I'd gathered to buy. "Now, Elise," I snap, my good mood soured.

"It's not even that bad," she tries to assure me, but the urge to change out of the stained dress is so strong. I plant more money than needed in her hand and insist she take our drinks to go.

When I get out to the car, I gasp in surprise at another porcelain doll waiting for me. This one isn't as fancy as the first, but I still like it. My ruined dress is no longer an issue as I snatch the doll and hug it to me, a part of me hoping it was from the gorgeous guy in the bookstore. A girl can dream.

CHAPTER SEVEN

~ Untrained ~

Benny

Tanner is busy. Doing what? I don't give a shit. It gives me a fucking breather. My rage still simmers under the surface after the turn of events with Kami. Three years, I've been by his side, doing his dirty work and feeling a bond I didn't know I was capable of, yet he's more of an enigma than a Victoria's Secret store.

I've been dying to see what my Bethany has been up to. Last night, it took the ultimate control not to snatch her right out of her doorway and drag her into my car. She'd been fucking exquisite in her silky nightgown that barely covered her ass. It was surreal that she opened the door and I got to view her in the flesh directly in my line of sight. I wanted to yank her lacy panties down her thighs and rub my dick along the crack of her ass. To feel her pure skin against mine.

To take.

Take.

Fucking take.

She belongs to me. Fated. A reincarnation.

But I'm wiser, because of Tanner.

I make smart moves, because of Tanner.

It was all worth the waiting. The motherfucking patience. Holding back when all I wanted to do was grab, grab, grab.

She dolled herself up.

Just for me.

And did a live feed.

Just for me.

I received the notification on my phone and watched as my sweet Bethany, my pretty goddamn new doll, looked right into the camera, right into my fucking soul, and spoke to me. Blew me a kiss that landed right on the tip of my cock. With haste, I yanked my dick out and jerked off, replaying her video over and over and over again until I shot my load all over her stunning face on the screen.

And the best news, according to Tanner—she has a twin. I'd seen her for myself, albeit muted by the darkness and Bethany blocking my full view of her. The girl was a sobbing mess. Watching the two Bethany girls bicker was fascinating as fuck. An illusion. Too perfect to be real. The ache that never stops throbbing in my chest intensified to an earth-shattering roar.

Two.

Two.

Two.

Mine.

Kami, even when forced to divulge details under Tanner's authoritative glare, still held back. One day, I'll cut her tongue from her throat and stomp it under my boot. If she doesn't want to speak, I'll make sure she can't motherfucking speak. What she did tell me, though, warmed my soul.

Elizabeth is a book nerd. Quiet. Shy. Detailed and organized. Childlike. Innocent.

Elise is a popular girl. Loud. Outgoing. Flighty and disorganized. Woman. Not-so-innocent.

Two sides of a single shiny coin.

I want both sides.

I want them both, goddammit.

Kami babbled on about shit. She had lots of information on Elise. Her likes, dislikes, favorite foods, music—I catalogued it all, but when I compared it to my list for Elizabeth, it was severely lacking. It pissed me off. Made me crave to discover those things on my own.

When I noticed the two girls leaving together this morning, I followed them to a quirky, half-priced vintage bookstore. Elise bounced in with irritating blonde streaks in her hair I hadn't noticed before, while Elizabeth followed meekly behind her. Elise wore holey jeans and an off-the-shoulder sweater that revealed too much skin. Elizabeth wore a simple white dress, modest and long-sleeved. Pure. The knee-highs were a nice touch. The pale pink headband in her gorgeous dark hair was an even nicer touch. The scuff-free black dress shoes on her feet made my dick hard.

Slipping into the store was difficult because of the stupid fucking bell on the door, but I eventually managed to push in behind a woman with three noisy children. People were so focused on the wailing toddler, they didn't notice me come in. The woman retreated from the store quickly after many annoyed glares from patrons.

Now, I'm looking for Elizabeth, but it's Elise whom I

find first. I peek between the top row of books on a shelf. Her ass jiggles as she motions to the menu board, flirting with the male barista. I want to strangle the asshole for the heated look he's giving her. My eyes scan the area, looking for Elizabeth.

"She's just had her heart broken, so go gentle on her." The voice is sweet, familiar, and I jerk around to face my obsession.

Pretty New Doll.
Bethany.
Mine.

She's fucking captivating. I stand there gaping at her, not wanting to blink and watch her disappear. She bites on her fat bottom lip that begs to be sucked as her gaze travels down to my neck, then my chest. A blush creeps across her throat as she inspects the new tattoos covering old scars. Tanner thought tattoos would help change my appearance. I think he just has a hard-on for tats.

Blinking away her daze, she waves at me, and my eyes fixate on her slender fingers, the nails painted a sweet bubblegum pink. "Hi. She's my sister." *And I'm your brother.*

I want to grab her by her tiny jaw and jerk her to my mouth. I want to inhale her, suck her, lick her, and fuck her.

I want her. I want her. I fucking want her.

"Right. Okay." The blush spreads up to her cheeks, and she turns to leave.

Not so fast, Pretty New Doll.

I strike out with my hand, snagging hers.

I want her. I want her. I fucking want her.

"Ouch." Her body jerks at my touch, and I release her,

then silently curse when I realize she's stabbed herself on my keychain. Her blood, bright and motherfucking brilliant, blooms like a rose on her pure skin.

I want her. I want her. I fucking want her.

"I'm sorry." My voice shakes, and I sound like a fucking idiot, but I don't care. My dream is standing before me, a picture of innocence—perfection personified.

Her nostrils flare and her mouth parts. Hazel eyes flicker with lust. With curiosity. With intrigue. With interest. My sweet, sweet doll's eyes are so fucking expressive. It makes me wonder what they'll look like when I have her pinned beneath me as I drive my cock into her untouched cunt. One shy, heated look from this girl and I know she's a virgin. That she's waited just for me. She wants me to take it. She wants me to push her frilly panties to the side and make her scream. Her eyes practically beg for it. This is how it should have been all those years ago. A fresh sprinkle of hate crawls over my skin for my father and mother.

Reaching out, I grasp her tiny hand. It's cool to the touch, and I want to kiss her until her flesh burns with heat. As if she's under my fucking spell, she watches as I bring her skinny finger to my mouth. I kiss the tiny blood rosebud and fire blazes within me, a hunger like never before clawing at me from the inside.

I need her. I need her. I fucking need her.

The urge to devour her nearly consumes me. It almost has me ignoring every lesson Tanner has ever taught me.

Almost.

With my eyes on her heated hazel ones, I suck the sweet, metallic blood from her finger. But it's not enough.

Like a motherfucking vampire, I want to suck it all from her body and fill her back up with me.

I need her. I need her. I fucking need her.

Her breath hitches when I lick her, soft but suggestive. The lick promises pleasure. It promises so much more than her world can give her. My tongue silently says, *"Soon, I'll save you, my Bethany."* It takes everything in me to pull her hand away from my greedy mouth, but I release her despite wanting to cage her forever.

I beam at her. "There. All better."

Her cheeks blaze crimson once more. My sweet Bethany loves my smiles. I'll smile at her as I fuck her over and over and fucking over again.

"Um…thank you?" Her words are breathless. Embarrassed even. So fucking adorable.

"You're beautiful."

Her lips twitch as she attempts to hide a smile. Pretty New Doll loves the attention. She practically glows, goddammit. Stunning. The motherfucking sun.

She swallows and jokes, "Says the man creeping on my sister from the shadows."

Her words cause my blood to run icy cold. The other girl—her twin—is nothing compared to her. Fucking nothing. Elizabeth is absolutely perfect. The other girl is flawed and damaged—used and broken. She needs restoring.

But this one?

This one needs nothing…but me.

"No." I grit my jaw. "She's not right. Her presence, the blonde, her attitude, it's all…wrong." I grin at her again, loving how she responds to me. "But you? You are perfect."

Her expressive hazel eyes peer straight inside me. For a brief moment, I'm afraid she'll see all the dark, dirty, shameful parts of me I don't want to face. My failures. My childish obsessions. My kinks and shortcomings.

But she doesn't seem to see any of it.

She sees me.

And I fucking see her too.

"I'll being *seeing* you," I tell her, my promise so thick, you could cut it. I steal one last glance at the angel in the bookstore before I slip away. This was supposed to be a recon mission, a moment to peek in on their lives and gather real intel—intel that cunt Kami couldn't provide. Instead, I ran right into her. The innocent little thing caught me right in the middle of my naughty act.

No judgment.

No anger.

She was smitten.

My heart swells as I stride out to my car. Once inside, I'm irritated Tanner is blowing up my phone.

Tanner: I checked up on your cells. I think you're going to like them.

Tanner: Where are you?

Tanner: Monster…

Tanner: Goddammit, you're stalking them, aren't you?

Tanner: Don't take them.

Tanner: Don't fucking take them.

Tanner: So help me, if you ruined all this because you couldn't fucking be patient…

I grin at the screen, elated as hell. This day has been like a shot of heroin straight to the vein. I'm buzzing with the thrill. My dick is alive with the need to possess and consume her.

Me: I didn't take them. I'm out grabbing a coffee. Calm your shit, man.

Tanner: Good boy.

My high fades, and I frown. I need to put a new plan in place. When I look back at the bookstore, my smile is back. Elise bounces from the store, a book clutched tightly in one hand and a to-go coffee in the other, while Elizabeth sits in the car already waiting for her. Elise climbs into the car, and her head moves as she babbles, basically carrying on a conversation with herself.

Elizabeth, my pretty new doll, is still in the moment with me. She looks over her shoulder and scans the cars as if seeking me out. Her hazel eyes search for me. The sun shines through the windows, highlighting her smooth pale face. The smile on her plump lips is a gift just for me.

As much as I want to roll down my window and call her over to my car so I can yank her in and take her now, I refrain. Barely. With my gaze forward, I hit the gas and drive away before I break all the rules and ruin everything.

She's worth the wait.

"You're keeping something from me." Tanner's voice carries a slight edge to it as he sips his bourbon from the tumbler in his iron grip. Everything about him screams calm, but I don't miss the flames flickering in his amber eyes or the way his knuckles turn white with how hard he's holding the glass.

"I'm not," I lie, careful to keep my voice even, my

stare on him steady.

He has no room to talk about keeping things from each other. Want to talk about Kami? Asshole.

He holds my gaze for a beat before rattling his glass and downing the rest. His fingers snap together, and a moment later, a curvy brunette is shoved into the room. Regaining her composure, she waltzes over to us. I'm not interested, but my dick has been at half-mast ever since I tasted my Bethany. Seeing long brown hair and full lips is almost enough for me to pretend it's her.

If I squint just the right way...

Reaching forward, I grab the bottle of bourbon from the table between us, pour three fingers worth into his glass, and bring the bottle to my lips. The brunette straddles his lap, but his blazing gaze is on me.

Master only bows for one.

I press my lips to the bottle and drink straight from it. Drink. Drink. Drink. Tanner's eyes are wide with surprise as I chug the liquor. As soon as the alcohol burns through me, I settle back, resting my head on the cushion behind me. Unbuckling my jeans, I tug my aching cock from its confines, close my eyes, and stroke myself. Tanner's eyes are on me—I don't have to see him to know they are. They always are. This little show is for him. A fucking distraction. A reminder that we are a team. That he needs me just as much as I need him. Make him need me more. Because fuck Kami.

"Sugar, my friend's cock needs attention," he growls to the woman before pushing her from his lap. Our gazes meeting for a brief moment.

Her bracelets jangle as she approaches, wariness

ablaze in her eyes. Her instincts are right, but she knows why she's here. The liquor is alive in my veins. And as long as I keep my eyes closed, I can pretend. So I do. I can keep up the charade that this dumb bitch is my Bethany until I have the real one beneath me. The thought of driving my cock inside her and destroying her hymen makes my cock jerk in my grip. I can hear shuffling. The tear of a condom. What surprises me is when a strong hand covers mine to still my stroking. Tanner slides the rubber down my shaft.

"Friends look out for friends," he assures me, lust thick in his voice.

Forcing my eyes open, I meet his gaze. If the devil had eyes, they would be Tanner's. Fire and fury and fucking ferocity rolled into amber orbs.

"Thanks, Master," I tell him, my tongue running along my bottom lip in a suggestive way.

His gaze darkens as evil lurks behind his eyes, and I wonder if he's ever felt this way about a man before. The need to touch rather than be touched. There is nothing submissive about Tanner, and if he thought I would, I'm sure he would bend me over and try to own me.

Not going to happen, my friend.

I do the owning around here.

"Of course, Monster." Sitting on the arm of my chair, he snaps his fingers, and the brunette obeys. Like the good little whore she is, she straddles my waist and the alcohol sets in, fast and hard. Through my haze, it's easier to mistake the brunette for my Bethany. Mind over matter. Her fingers work at tugging my shirt up off my chest, and I assist, tossing my shirt at Tanner, who remains silent as he watches.

Her eyes expand as she takes in the ink covering the entire right side of my chest and torso. The scars beneath raise the scales on the monster, making it almost appear like he's moving over my skin with each breath I take.

"Tell me you've been looking for me," I demand, my hands all over the brunette's firm tits. She smells sweet. Not perfect, but tasty. When she sinks down on my cock, I groan. This bitch feels like a whore. Loose as fuck. It ruins the fantasy and the need to end her is overwhelming. I want to destroy the wrong, ruined dolly.

"Don't think, Monster," Tanner's smooth voice says as it washes over me like a warm blanket. "Just pretend. Not for much longer. Soon, she'll be all yours. You can suck her and fuck her and make her bleed."

A moan escapes me as I recall her sweet metallic taste. The way her breath hitched when I sucked her poor injured finger. When I finally have her, I want to taste her blood again. When I shatter her innocence, perhaps I'll lap up the remnants as it trickles from her perfect pussy, running down to the crack of her apple-shaped ass.

"That's it," Tanner encourages. He's behind me now, his strong, capable fingers kneading out knots in my shoulders I didn't know existed. Like the devil, he whispers things into my left ear. But instead of having a voice of reason on my right, he whispers dark things there too. "Take her. Use her."

My hips thrust up into the wannabe doll as Tanner's teeth graze at my left earlobe. Large palms splay over my pectoral muscles before reaching out to cover my hands over her tits. I squeeze hard, eliciting a cry of pain. With his hot breath in my ear and palms greedy to touch me as I touch her, I let the alcohol steal me away. I let the brunette help create a fantasy. I let the pleasure take over.

"Turn around," he rasps, his order to her no doubt heard.

The practiced whore swivels around so her ass faces me without breaking her stride of sliding up and down on my shaft. I don't want to look at her ass. I'm afraid the spell will be broken if I open my eyes.

"Finger your pretty new doll's ass," he instructs, his hot breath making my dick jolt inside her loose hole.

I bring two fingers to his mouth, and he sucks them past his lips, his tongue eager to taste me. Five bucks says if I asked him to put his mouth on my dick, he'd bow before me.

Master only bows to one.

He'd suck my cock and worship it.

I'd own him.

I already do.

I own him because the promise of more is something he desperately wants but will never ask for. It's my duty to tease and lure and slowly drag him to me. I want him on his knees, but not to suck my dick. I want him to want to so badly, he bows to me. I want him on his knees—that's where all my obsessions belong.

Right.

In.

Fucking.

Front.

Of.

Me.

I want to stroke them and praise them and adore

them from beneath me.

Owning him in such a way would feed me. Imagine the power that would give me.

Yanking my fingers from his mouth with a pop, I find the crack of the brunette's ass. When I shove the two fingers inside her without warning, she whimpers, but like the eager cunt she is, picks up her pace as she fucks me. Her ass has been used before, and it loosens to the fit of my fingers. I add another two without lubing them, forcing them inside. A pained groan spills from her lips as she tilts farther forward, giving me more access. Tucking my thumb into my palm, I curl my fingers into a fist and push inside her up to my wrist. The sounds coming from her are not ones of pleasure. It fucking hurts. Good. I quite like wearing her like a puppet master with his worthless puppet.

"Good boy," Tanner breathes against my neck. "My monster is learning. Taking. Owning."

Master only bows to one.

I angle my head to the right, exposing my neck to him. An offering. A morsel. A motherfucking taste of what he desires most. His hesitation is brief, but then his full lips open and close over the crook between my shoulder and throat. I expect kissing and sucking, but pain penetrates the haze of alcohol and lust. His teeth sink into me, biting, and warm liquid runs down from my neck over my chest. He's a ravenous beast. Starved for me. Just as he should be. But he's marking me. Taking ownership.

That's my job, motherfucker.

I fuck the whore's ass with my fist, forcing her body over my cock with the pounding of her asshole. Blood mixed with a hint of shit seeps down to my elbow. My nuts are tight with the need to come. It would be so much better if I had my Bethany, but the wait won't be forever.

Soon.

Soon, my pretty new doll.

Soon.

Tanner's greedy mouth isn't satisfied with just my neck. He wants more. His teeth linger by the flesh of my jaw, and he digs his fingers into my cheeks, turning my head. For a hot moment, his breath mingles with mine. I risk opening my eyes, and am so glad I do. His fiery need is so fucking desperate, it sends me over the edge. I love the power I have over him. So simple. So addicting. He wants to latch his lips to mine and prod me with his tongue, spearing inside my mouth. The intrusion would be forceful and demanding, much like my little master doll in all aspects of his life. He wants to kiss me as though he owns me. But I have him by the proverbial balls.

"Fuck," he groans against my mouth, our lips nearly touching. "Fuck, Monster."

The way he growls out his words, the way my pretend dolly's body is forced to rub up and down along my cock—I finally lose it. My eyes snap shut, and I see her.

Elizabeth.

My Bethany.

Pretty New Doll.

She's a delight all in white.

A motherfucking princess.

My queen.

I come and come and come, filling the whore with my desires for another. I've barely stopped spurting out my release when the brunette is jerked from me. I'm wasted from the liquor and high off the fantasy, but blood and shit coats my entire arm. Fucking disgusting whore.

Monster is sated.

And Master is still hungry.

Wrenching her around, he shoves her down between my thighs on her knees. "Pull the condom off and suck him clean," he snarls, his grip in her dark hair brutal.

My cock has fallen limp, but the way he makes her cry out has me hardening again. She clumsily removes the condom, and he releases her long enough to push his slacks down his thighs and sheath his cock with a rubber. His eyes on mine, he lifts her by the hips and drives deep into her primed cunt. It satisfies me knowing he wants to feel where my cock just was. Her squeals remind me of pigs headed for slaughter, and his fist is back in her hair, forcing her on my cock.

I'm amused and turned on by the way he brutalizes her. She's not real. She's a fucking whore. A loose cunt. A nightmare when all I can focus on is my dream.

Tanner pounds into her hard enough she screams around my hard dick, the vibration making my balls tighten. It makes the hairs on my bare lower abs stand on end. Those screams wake the beast—anger the beast—feed the beast.

"You like this?" he grunts out, his eyes wild with lust as he regards me. "Are you happy, Monster?"

I'll be happy when you're on your knees worshipping me, Master.

"Hold her hands."

His command comes out as more of a beg, and it

takes everything in me not to smirk at him. Instead, I obey, gripping her wrists as he pulls his blade from his jacket pocket. Flipping open the knife, he stares right at me. Tanner has lost it. He's out of control, raging like the beast that often claims me. Lust, rage, and jealousy blaze in his eyes as he lifts her head slightly so my cock is out of harm's way when he digs the blade into the side of her throat. He slices along her carotid without apology before pulling the blade free and roaring when her wound spurts like a greedy cunt squirting out its release. His eyes remain on mine as she gurgles just above my cock, her weight pushing her farther onto me. The heat from her blood rushes down around me like a waterfall of lust, and I work my dick back into her mouth now that she's hardly able to fight me, being nearly dead and all.

I come down her throat.

Jesus Christ, do I come, and Tanner's eyes blaze like the flames of hell when the creamy release taints the blood pouring from the hole he created.

Tanner comes too.

Together, we grunt like two wild animals, our kill bleeding out between us.

His stare makes claims. *Mine. Mine. Mine.*

The obsession Tanner harnesses is dangerous. Enough to endanger my pretty new doll if he doesn't contain it. I'll have to scale back. Keep him on a tight leash. Teach the master how *not* to be a motherfucking monster.

It takes time.

You must exercise patience.

Tanner's words, not mine.

I'm just the one who obeys those simple rules.

I will win.

I will keep them all.

My perfect, precious dolls.

Mine.

Tanner pulls out of the dead whore and lazily pushes her to the floor. Her face slides down my thigh, thudding against the floor between my legs. His manic eyes zero in on my blood soaked cock, the crimson river dripping between my hard thighs. Like a bull in the motherfucking arena, he charges, his greedy, needy hands swiping at the mess.

Cum.

Blood.

Saliva.

His fingers run through the river like he's going to finger-paint the goddamn walls with it. He kicks the dead doll away with a heavy boot and takes her place. Standing like a seething dragon over me, he loses himself to the blood, my seed, *me*. And I let him. I allow him to indulge in this chaotic moment, studying his breathing, the tick of his jaw, the flickering in his eyes.

Obsession.

With me.

Master only bows to one.

My cock twitches once more, and his hands are no longer curious, but full of intent. Laying back, I enjoy the way he worships the blood, smearing it up my abs and onto my chest, then my cock, the fake doll's blood still dripping from it. The intense pleasure coursing through me has nothing to do with the need to come and everything to do with the need to possess and own.

His hands leave me and he fists his own hard cock, stroking over and over again, until cum explodes in ribbons of his thick, creamy release. I flinch when it lands over my cock.

And his spine stiffens.

Abrupt. Sudden. Sharp.

Reality seeps back in as the blood soaks the cushion beneath me and I use my shirt to quickly remove his mark.

Neither of us say a word as he jerks his hand away from his cock as though he's been burned. *You can't burn the devil, silly.* Rising to his full height, he yanks his slacks up, and glares at me.

He's retreating.

And I need him to stay.

So I pull the leash.

Tug. Tug. Tug. Just like he wants to be tugging on my fat cock.

Running my fingers through the blood on my abdomen, I bring it to my lips and suck it off. His eyes burn through me as he watches. Tanner's favorite color is red. Tanner's favorite color is me.

Red. Red. Red.

When I have all my dollies in a row, I'll make sure to get him a shiny red bowtie to wear.

"Want to go to Waffle House? I'm fucking hungry," I say, as if none of this just happened and he didn't witness my rejection of him owning me.

Monsters don't have feelings.

Monsters don't want power.

Monsters don't try to outsmart their master.

Authority has his spine straightening and shoulders

squaring. *Whatever you need, Master, to make you feel better.* He forces a playful smile, but I know it's difficult when he's already bared the belly to his beast. Offered his fattest vein for me to sink my teeth into. A master is nothing but a bossy man in a suit compared to a beast who decimates and devours.

"Your treat, asshole," he grunts.

We both laugh, this time not forced at all.

Tanner always buys.

CHAPTER EIGHT

~ *Virgin* ~

Dillon

There's not enough coffee in the world to keep me alert today.

"Rough night?" Marcus huffs, throwing himself into my chair, forcing me to frown and sit on the corner of my desk. I do a quick once over of his fancy suit and roll my eyes. Is he going to run for congress or some shit?

"Jade is in her horny-as-sin stage of pregnancy," I mutter, and his brows lift almost to his hairline.

"Is that a thing?"

"Well, my dick can agree it is. I'm fucking chafed from her riding me so much."

Picking up a pen, he throws it at me, and I catch it, holding it up. "What the hell?"

"No man should ever complain about getting too much ass," he grumbles. "Go write up a ton of paperwork and then bitch to me."

My eyes dart to his face, noticing the bags forming under his eyes. "You been here all night?"

Pushing back in the chair to stretch, he rubs his hands over his face before answering. "My night didn't go as planned, so I came in to catch up on some of those interviews from the club workers."

"Anything you need to tell me?"

He rolls his eyes. "Do I look like a tween girl who needs to discuss my feelings?"

I kick out my leg, hitting his ankle. "You sound like one, and although I love hearing about your social life, I was referring to the interviews."

He sits forward, smiling half-heartedly. "Shit, sorry. I'm just tired."

"No problem," I grunt. *Join the club.*

"One dancer. She mentioned something about a man she recognized from a different club who came in and had a heated discussion with Mr. Law. Said she only saw him because she walked into his office during the talk."

"Did she have a name for us?"

He grabs a folder he must have put on my desk and thumbs through it. "No name, but an address for a club called The Vault. She said she applied for a job there but was turned down."

A groan leaves my chest. "You think she's just disgruntled and this is her way of getting back?"

"Either way, it's the only lead we have, so it's worth looking into."

"Did you run the club?"

"Yeah. It's owned by a Cassian Harris."

Getting to my feet, I pull on my jacket and grab the car keys. "Priors?"

Marcus follows behind me, matching my stride. "Nothing. Not even a parking ticket. He is squeaky clean."

"Too clean, or just a top member of society?" I snort.

"Let's go find out."

The Vault has a completely different atmosphere from the one owned by the victim of some crazed murderer. A woman greets us at the front, asking to see our card and then to sign in, like we're at a spa or some shit. When I show her my badge, she smiles and walks us to the real leather couches situated along the walls. "If you take a seat, I'll inform management you are here." She beams, offering us both a drink while we wait.

"Thank you?" I reply, unsure if there's a reason she's being so polite. Usually workers are standoffish when we flash our badge. Marcus sits, and I decide to do the same. There are two sets of double doors, one on each side of the "welcome desk," and I wonder what's beyond them.

The floor looks like it's made of cracked glass, and it reflects the light from a giant chandelier hanging from the ceiling, igniting the foyer in a brilliant bright light. Men enter in thousand dollar suits, then disappear behind large black doors. My eyes find Marcus, who nods his head. This place is in a league of its own and shouldn't really care about a club like Rebel's Reds. I doubt there's any real rivalry between them. A door made with a mirror effect, much like the wall and floor, opens from beside me. It was so camouflaged, I didn't even realize there was a door there.

"Detectives." A tall, well-dressed man stands in front of me, offering his hand first to me, then Marcus. His tone is deep, authoritative. There are no nerves in his mannerisms. He is cool, collected, and it puts me on motherfucking edge.

"Would you like to come through to my office?"

"Yes, thank you," Marcus answers for us, following him through the same door he came from. The mirror theme continues down the corridor, and my eyes sweep the long hall as we pass a few doors before he finally enters one.

It's small and holds no personality. No pictures of family. No computer or other electronics. It's barren except for a desk with chairs on either side of it.

He takes his seat, then gestures for us to take the others.

Marcus gets out his notepad and pencil. "Can I confirm who you are?"

The guy tilts his head, regarding us. His eyes are the color of honey, but there is nothing sweet about the way they bore into us, stripping away the layers.

"I own this establishment," he retorts, clasping his hands together and leaning his elbows on the desk.

"So, you're Cassian Harris?" I clarify.

"Yes."

"Mr. Harris, we are investigating the murder of a Maximus Law. Can you tell me how you know him?" Marcus asks.

I smile internally at the way Marcus posed the question. Not *if* you know him, but *how*.

"I'm sorry," Mr. Harris says. "I feel at a disadvantage." He smiles, but his eyes are vacant. My sixth sense sends a chill up my spine.

"A disadvantage?" Marcus asks.

"Yes, you know who I am, yet you haven't informed

me of who you are."

Jackass.

Pulling out my badge, I smack it down on the table in front of him. He looks it over with intense scrutiny before a twitch in his lip makes my piss boil. He's a game player. It's a good damn thing I'm fucking headstrong and have played with the big leagues.

He ignores Marcus as he flashes his badge, only having eyes for me.

"Detective Scott. What can I do for you?"

I slip my badge into the pocket of my slacks and lean back in the chair to show him his little show doesn't rattle me. "You can answer the question. How do you know Maximus Law?"

"You mean, *knew* Maximus Law?"

Swallowing the growl, I smirk. I'm aching to smack his head into the goddamn table. "We have reason to believe you saw him the night of his death."

Leaning back, he taps a finger to his forehead, then asks, "Which night did he die?"

Fucker is smarter than I gave him credit for.

"The nineteenth," Marcus answers for me.

"Well, I was here all day and night on the nineteenth."

"Do you not need to check your schedule?" I grind out.

He eyes me, a spark igniting in his unusually colored eyes. "I can keep track of the days, Detective. The nineteenth was a Thursday, and on Thursdays, I see to the accounts, then spend the evenings unwinding inside a warm body."

I refrain from rolling my eyes. "Can anyone verify

that for you?"

A wicked grin spreads over his face. "Of course." Pulling his cell from his pocket, he dials a number and brings the phone to his ear.

"Kami, office B. Now."

"While we wait, would you mind telling us why a witness said she saw you at Rebel's Reds?"

"A witness said this, Detective Scott?" He says my name like it's a swear word. "It's not a crime to visit other establishments. I was merely scouting out purchase opportunities. I'm looking to expand."

"So, you were there to buy the club?" I demand, my patience wearing thin.

He wags a finger and shakes his head. "No, quite the contrary. The place wasn't nearly worth my time, so I thanked Mr. Law and left."

"Were you aware of Mr. Law's involvement in trafficking women?"

A brazen question for this early on in the investigation, but I want to see the look on his face. He gives me not one tell as to whether he knows or not.

The door opens and a young girl in a pair of khakis and a tank top enters. She's petite with pink streaky hair, her eyes huge and expressive. She immediately walks over to where Harris is sitting and crawls into his lap, facing us.

Fucking creepy.

"Can you confirm your whereabouts Thursday the nineteenth?" Marcus asks, hoping to catch Harris out by not asking her straight out if she was with him.

"Who the fuck are you?" She cocks her brow, and her attitude makes a laugh bubble from my chest. She reminds me of Jade when we first started working together.

Marcus recoils, shooting his gaze my way. He doesn't like brash, mouthy women. He prefers a chick to act like one.

Harris wraps a hand around her waist, his fingers breaching the waistline and disappearing down past her pelvis. She gasps when he touches her pussy, and Marcus shifts in his seat, getting uncomfortable. Harris is a power player. He thinks this will undermine us and make us want to leave, but he's a fool if he thinks I don't know these tactics. "Where was I Kami? Don't be coy," he teases.

"He was with me."

Pulling his hand from her pants, he pushes her from his lap before smacking her ass and gesturing for her to leave.

"We need her name and a testimony confirming your alibi on record. Just a formality," Marcus informs him, his eyes narrowing further.

"I hope you have more than that to warrant you being here," Harris states in a bored tone.

"We're just following all leads and ruling out possible suspects," I growl with a smile on my face.

"Well, Detective Scott, I'm a businessman, not a murderer. If Mr. Law was trafficking women, it's more than likely a deal gone wrong. Tricky business, and not one I dabble in."

I get to my feet, and Marcus follows suit, offering his hand to Harris. "Thank you for your time."

"Glad to assist you in any way I can."

As we leave, Marcus pulls a handkerchief from his pocket and begins rubbing his hand on it, a scowl on his face. I want to rib him for owning an old man snot rag, but he's having a meltdown.

"I didn't think when I went in for the handshake…" He shudders, shaking his head.

"It's just pussy, Marcus. It's not a virus."

"How the fuck do I know what she's carrying?" he snaps. "She clearly works here. God only knows how many men she lets handle her there."

As we make our way back to the car, I nod my head at his vagina cloth. "You aren't bringing that in the car."

"It's my grandpa's," he grumbles. "He's eighty-eight. I can't throw it away." He frowns, stuffing it in his pocket.

I grin. "That's the most pussy he's had in a while."

"Fuck you, man." He fastens his seatbelt and looks over at me. "So, this was a bust."

My eyes scan the huge structure of the club. It's massive, and we didn't even get to look around inside. Something is off for sure with that fucker. Wealth and owning this type of business can leave a man very cocksure, and I hope that's all it is. My intuition, however, tells me there is much more to him and it's not the last time we're going to be seeing him.

It's been a long ass day and we still have nothing to go on. I spent the entire afternoon looking into Cassian Harris and anyone he's associated with. The further I dug, the more suspicious I became being that there's nothing on this guy. No past. No ties to anyone. His title is on documents for a few more properties, but that's it. Even asking informants and people into that scene, the name Cassian was unknown. He ran an empire, but no one knew of him. People gave different names for who they thought owned his club, but no one would or could confirm if this was the same guy we spoke to. Someone who stays anonymous and uses different names always has something to hide. And that fucker isn't getting off my radar that easily.

My cell vibrates against my leg and a text from Jade lights the screen.

Jade: Left MJ's doll at Beth's and she is screaming for it, but I'm midway through cooking dinner. Would you please stop by and pick it up on your way home?

Starting the engine, I send a quick reply and make my way to the twins' house.

The sun is going down. I love this time of day, right on the cusp of night. My thoughts are with Scarlet, the worker from Rebel's Reds who brought up she recognized the owner of The Vault. He appears to be more of a ghost than someone who would do his own interviewing, so why would she remember him?

Tomorrow, I'm taking a picture of Cassian Harris to her to see if it's even him she was talking about. Maybe it was someone else from his club. Maybe it's nothing.

Whatever it is, I'm going to figure it the fuck out.

CHAPTER NINE

~ *Unused* ~

Benny

Tanner enters the office he lets me use, steam almost pouring from his ears. It's so rare to see him lose his usual cool demeanor.

"I'm waiting for a call back, then I will have a job for you tonight," he barks.

My thoughts go to Dillon and seeing him on the video monitor in the lobby. When I first saw him, my heart rate picked up pace, almost beating from my chest. My hand went straight for my faithful knife, and I had to will my erratic thoughts to calm so I didn't march out there and turn Tanner's lobby into a blood bath.

Seeing Dillon brought the reality home that, as of late, my thoughts haven't strayed to my dirty doll. Not once has she crept into my mind. Instead, Bethany has taken up all the room. She's burrowed herself under my skin and cleansed me—washed away the urge to take back my dirty little doll. She will always belong to me. I still love her and would take her, but she's not where my every waking thought lies anymore. My heart feels free from the grip she once had over me. She was so special and perfect, but she hurt me by running and forced my hand too many times. I don't think I will ever leave the debt she owes me behind. Her betrayal comes with a price, and she will have to pay it. But for now…for now, I won't take her life. I'll leave her until the time is right. I will take my sweet Bethany and lock the world out, shutting us away—together.

"Benjamin? Did you hear a word I said?"

No.

"Yes. You have a job for me."

"Your father was always great to have as an ally, but he's not my only inside man. My informant warned me someone saw me at Rebel's Reds and spilled their guts to the detectives on the case. He's getting me the name and address of the loose-lipped fucker who brought the detectives to my. Fucking. Safe. Haven." His jaw clenches and nostrils flare. "And, Benjamin?" I give him my attention, enjoying the rage rising off him and blanketing me. "I want her tongue. Make it hurt. This isn't for pleasure."

"Noted."

I wait for the flurry of excitement at seeing my dirty doll.

Rage.

Thrill.

Overwhelming need and desire.

Instead, my heart is corroded with the acid of what she once was and what she did to me. My focus easily leaves her and fixates on my breathtaking Bethany. She is waving goodbye to Dirty Doll and pauses, looking around at her surroundings. She wraps her arms around her waist, and instead of going inside, she begins walking down the path to the street.

I start the engine and slowly follow her. The material of the flowing purple dress she wears caresses her body with each stride while the wind picks up the soft strands of her dark hair, blowing them around her shoulders and across her face.

She walks for a good twenty minutes before entering the small town and coming to a stop in front of a movie theater. A crowd has gathered outside, and I recognize the wrong Bethany amongst the herd. A lanky boy with a leering grin steps forward to greet my perfect new doll and her body retracts. She steps out of his reach, her brows furrowing. His gaze darts to her sister, who just shrugs, and mouths, "Come on, Beth."

Bethany is visibly shaken at seeing the ugly boy. Her entire demeanor changes with a quick flip of a switch.

"Screw you, Elise!" Bethany shouts, turning on her heel and abandoning her plans.

Stepping from the car, I walk along the opposite path just as she crosses the road and heads straight for me. Her head is down staring at her feet. I know she hasn't seen me when she almost knocks into me, sidestepping around me at the last minute without lifting her gaze. My breath stills as I debate reaching out for her, but, as if sensing me, she stops moving and looks back over her shoulder. Her hazel eyes bore straight into mine. It's as if the entire world halts and the moment is suspended in time, two souls searching, surging, connecting.

"Bookshop stalker?" she questions in astonishment, a wide smile—just for me—playing at her lips. The world rights itself and my inner boy mirrors her smile.

"Beautiful bleeder," I respond, then cringe when her face blanches. A moment later, she bursts into musical filled laughter, and it's stunning.

"That's a new one."

She looks back to the crowd across the street, then to me again. The sun is beginning to set, and the woman I'm supposed to kill comes to mind, along with her address and work schedule. The order from Tanner was to take care of it *now*, but for *now*, it can wait. I have something more important to tend to.

"Where are you heading?" I ask.

Biting her bottom lip, she clasps her hands together. "Home." Her shoulders lift in a shrug as she peers up at me through her thick lashes. "I guess."

I stare at her lips for a long moment. "Can I walk you?"

"Um…sure," she breathes, blushing a perfect red that spans over her porcelain pale skin and down her neck.

I offer my hand out to her, and when her small, supple hand slips into mine, my chest expands with a contentment I haven't felt in what feels like forever. Her scent wafts over me with every movement we take, and I can almost taste it.

Sweet and ripe.

"I love the color of your skin," I tell her, holding up our joined hands and bringing hers to my lips. Her eyes widen as she looks up at me.

"My sister says I should tan." She half smiles.

"No. Don't ever do that." My tone is harsher than intended, and I worry about frightening her off, but instead, find her studying me with fondness.

"I won't. I promise," she assures me, her tone soft and breathless.

I squeeze her hand tighter. "Your sister tries too hard to be like them."

"Like who?" Her brows crinkle together in confusion.

"Everyone else. She could get lost in a sea of people and no one would be able to pick her out, but you..." I study Bethany intently, "you...your beauty is a stark contrast. Perfect in every way. You're like a brand-new porcelain doll, never been taken from her packaging."

Her gasp brings my feet to a stop, and she tugs her hand from mine, then folds her arms over her chest, offering me a guarded smile. Questions sit on the tip of her tongue, but she refrains from asking. Her eyes are narrowed as she studies me, and I wonder if she's figured out I'm the one who gifted her the doll.

"Did I say something wrong?"

Shaking her head, she tells me, "No, it's just...this is my house." She nods her head, gesturing to the house behind her. I was so lost in her, I hadn't realized how fast or long we had been walking.

"Oh," I say, offering a tight smile. I don't want her to go inside. I want to stay in her presence forever.

She will be mine.

Mine.

Mine.

"I'd ask you inside for coffee, but my mother is home."

I look up at the dark house knowing full well no one is within its confines right now. She doesn't want me to come inside. Have I scared her? The porcelain doll comment most certainly clued her in, and now, I've frightened her. Disappointment floods through me.

"Maybe another time?" I state.

There will definitely be a next time, Pretty New Doll.

"Do you have a phone?" she blurts as I'm turning to leave.

My heart dances in my chest. "Yes." Pulling it from my pocket, I hand it to her, hoping she doesn't snoop through it and just adds her number. She flits her thumbs over the screen and hands it back to me. Looking down at the contact, my insides combust. On one hand, I want to stand here with her forever. But on the other, I want to take her and keep her from everyone.

Doll
1-555-433-5212

She knows. Bethany has to know I gave her the doll. Pushing the cell into my pocket, my elation is bustling through my veins and has my hands reaching out to cup her cheeks. Her breath hitches when I lower my head to meet her plump, fat lips. Her hands latch on to my wrists, and her lips part, filling my mouth with her fruity breath. A sigh escapes her as she closes her eyes. I taste her, flicking my tongue into her waiting, needy mouth, devouring and exploring every inch. She's warm and inviting, and my cock strains knowing her pussy will feel just as wet, just as hot—just as fucking perfect.

Her small tits push against my forearms making me want to tear the dress from her and claim her right there on the fucking lawn. My father's lawn. I plan to write him a letter when I return home tonight. *Time for an update, Daddy Dearest.*

A car door slamming pulls Bethany from my grip.

Looking past me, she stiffens. "Oh, hey, Dillon," she squeaks.

Every muscle in my body recoils.

Fuck.

Fuck.

Fuck.

Knowing it will leave me with no choice but having to kill him and take Bethany now, with no plan fully in place for her yet, I don't turn around. "I'll call you," I whisper against her ear before taking off, back toward where I left my car.

"You're not going to introduce yourself?" he bellows to the back of my head, but I just keep walking, hoping he doesn't follow. "Hey!" he shouts to my retreating form. "What's with that?" I hear him say, but it's muted in the distance. He isn't following, and I didn't fuck everything up by changing the plan. The rules. Tanner's rules.

I stake out Rebel's Reds. Tonight is the reopening after being shut down by the cops. Something about an investigation into the owner over sex trafficking. I'm not sure. Don't know and don't care. I never ask Tanner for details on the people he needs me to take care of. And same with the manager of this place. Tanner told me to kill Law, so I did.

I check for cameras, or more importantly, lack thereof. Tanner wanted me to make it as painful for this woman as possible. He claims she's the one who ratted us out to the cops, but my high from tasting my new doll has me wanting to get this over and done with so I can go home and see to the raging hard-on that hasn't gone down since leaving her.

What Tanner doesn't know can't hurt him. I'll tell him I choked her on my cock before cutting her lying tongue from her head and making her drown on her own blood.

Creeping across the lot, I pin my body against the building and slip behind an open door to the back of the club. Checking my watch, I wait for her to finish. A man comes out talking on his phone about the new guy who has taken over things being a dick. He smokes two cigarettes while he whines and bitches, and I think about killing him just to keep myself from having to inhale the disgusting smoke. Just as I'm about to alert him to my presence, he goes back inside.

"Bye, Jack," a woman's voice says as she steps into the night.

It's her—the woman from the photograph Tanner gave me.

I sneak up behind her, grasping each side of her head and snapping her neck before she can finish her startled screech. Pulling my knife from my pocket, I bend over her fallen body and pull her tongue from her open mouth, slicing it from her and dropping it into a small plastic bag. Opening one of the trashcans, I toss her inside. The lid refuses to close the first time, so I have to wrestle the thing, wedging her farther down inside. Just as I'm about to make my getaway, Jack returns. He eyes me, his features crashing in confusion before his gaze drops to the blood on my shirt, then the bag in my hand.

Fuck.

The cigarette falls from his lips as I move fast, swiping

the blade from my pocket and jabbing him in the neck with it. His eyes widen and his hands go to the spurting wound. Bringing his hands away, he looks at the blood with disbelief before dropping like a concrete block to the floor. Tossing him in the dumpster is going to be a harder task—one I'm not entertaining. He can stay there.

I make it back to my car and hit the gas.

"Lucy," I bark into the monitor, entering The Vault through the back and stripping out of my clothes in the small, tiled, wall-to-wall room. The light bleeps above the door, and a cleaner comes inside, bagging up my shit. I push through the door and move down the corridor to the back office I only learned existed when Tanner took me there to meet his Kami. Even thinking her name leaves a bad taste in my mouth.

"Benjamin, you shouldn't go in there," Lucy screeches, chasing after me. I halt, and her footfalls cease behind me. Looking over my shoulder, I give her a warning stare. Her bright blue eyes flicker with the urge to stop me—as if she ever could—but something in my glare has her taking pause. Holding her hands up in defeat, she murmurs, "I did warn you."

I burst through the door, and drop the bag that holds the dead girl's tongue.

Inside the weird glass box is Kami, her body bare of all clothing. She's covered in bruises and cuts, her flesh a canvas of blood and pain. Her tits strain against the glass as Tanner pounds into her pussy, and…he's naked. I've never seen him out of all his clothes before. His body ripples and strains with raw power. Natural tanned skin stretches over hard muscle, his forearms wrapped around her neck, holding her in a sort of headlock. And despite her many injuries, she screams in pleasure.

Her eyes land on me through the glass, and a devilish grin lifts her swollen lips.

"You're a vile, cunt. I fucking hate fucking you. You disgust me, you dirty whore!" he shouts as he powers into her, almost lifting her from the floor. He's so devoted to his lust, he doesn't even notice me in the room. My heart shrivels inside its habitat, all the power I once thought I held fleeing me, laughing in mockery. I don't own him. She does.

Pulling from her, he spins her body to face him and backhands her across the face. She spits blood as her head twists to the side. Her hand comes up in retaliation, but it's lacking momentum. She's tired and weaker than him. His eyes flare as he regards her. Wrapping his hand around her small neck, he lifts her clear from the floor and pins her against the glass, her head reaching a height well above his. I notice marks over his body—cuts, bruises, claw marks. The floor of their fuck cell is littered with weapons—knives, batons, and sex toys.

"I win," he tells her as her body stops fighting his hold and begins to go limp. "Don't tire out on me yet, my precious pain-whore." He releases her body, and she drops to the floor with a thwack. Her body jerks as she coughs and spits out more blood.

"You broke a tooth," she chokes out.

He grins down at her. "I'll make you an appointment at the dentist. Now, stop your fucking yapping and open that dirty mouth up." Her lips part, and he fists his thick, hard cock. I've never seen it this hard before, straining, veins bulging. His eyelids lower as he regards her and strokes over himself. "Fuck your whore hole for me, Kami. I won this time."

Her hand splays over the floor, pulling a purple fake cock toward her. She spits blood onto the tip, then lowers the device between her legs. She bristles at first, then her heavy pants match his. The sound of skin slipping over skin and her rotten wet cunt slurping with each thrust travels through the room, bouncing off the walls.

Fuck, I hate her.

They've ruined everything.

I was on such a high.

Cum pulses from Tanner straight into her waiting mouth. He wrings his cock dry, then holds his hand over her mouth. "Swallow like a good girl. Let me own you inside and out."

Fuck her.

Fuck him.

I leave the room.

Leave them.

Leave him.

CHAPTER TEN

~ *Uncontaminated* ~

Elizabeth

I'M BUZZING.
Flying on a cloud.
That kiss. Oh. My. God. It was everything. I've never been kissed so intensely before, like I was the most important person on the planet. His brown eyes shone with desire—desire I wanted to lick and burn my flesh. Dillon, God love him, really ruined my magical moment.

My chat with Dillon was a blur. I don't even recall what he said. Something about checking in to stop Jade from worrying over me rattling around the house alone again. Luckily for me, Mom wasn't long behind him. He chatted with her for a bit while I just pretended to listen. In reality, I didn't hear a word. I was in a daze. I desperately checked my phone every three seconds, and Dillon watched me with narrowed eyes. I knew he was curious about my new beau, but I wasn't divulging. A girl never kisses and tells. And this felt too special. I wanted to keep it just for me. Like if I spoke about it, people would judge and dampen this swirling euphoria coursing through my nerve endings. I've read about people having a connection and that insta-love you get in some romance novels. I was always aware it was fiction—only rumored to be possible. But if the tingles racing up my spine and buzzing of what feels like electricity warming and zapping through my entire nervous system isn't the proof of such connections, I don't know what is.

After a long, hot shower where my thoughts replayed the kiss over and over again, I lock myself in my room. I have no missed calls or texts. Disappointment surges through me. With a sigh, I open my bedroom window and lean out. The warm air whips around me, and my robe opens, baring my breasts to the dark trees flanking our property. Biting my lip, I tug my robe back around me. I'm still searching the darkness when my phone buzzes. Rushing over to it, I sit on the bed.

Elise: You really hurt Jason's feelings running off like that. He's a good guy who actually likes you. I wish you'd give him a chance.

Disappointment followed by extreme irritation floods through me as I tap out my response.

Me: He's not my type.

Elise: What IS your type?

I close my eyes, recalling my kiss from earlier. The way he consumed me in a way Jason would never be capable of.

Me: Tall. Dark hair. Muscular. Tattoos. Handsome. Mature. Someone who kisses me as though I'm their everything.

The three dots move as she replies. I can almost sense her rolling her eyes.

Elise: Good luck. Guys like that don't exist.

I want to tell her they do, that I kissed one tonight, but I decide against it. Elise will just rain on my parade. She'll taint my moment with her "big sister" advice and know-it-all self.

Me: Still not interested in Jason. Never will be, so drop it. Night.

My gaze flits over to my desk and my eyes bug out of my head when I see a new doll sitting beside the other two. He's been in my room. Dillon would flip his shit if he knew…which is exactly why he never can. Heat floods through me. The new doll being in my room should creep me out, but instead, I find it sweet. Three dolls from my stalker. My bookstore stalker. At least, I hope it's him.

She doesn't respond back for a long time. When my phone buzzes again, I expect to see Elise texting, but it's a number I don't recognize. My heart flutters like a butterfly hovering over a flower it so desperately wants to land on.

Unknown: I wish our kiss didn't have to end.

Heat burns across my skin as though I've stepped in front of a blazing fire. I walk back over to the window and stare out into the trees. My eyes strain as I look for movement. I think I see something white, but my mind is probably playing tricks on me. Defeated, I sit back down on my bed.

Me: I liked it entirely too much. What's your name?
Unknown: My friends call me Monster.

I frown. He's far from a monster. He's like one of those hot guardian angels you read about in romance novels. Alpha and giant and strong. Handsome to a fault. His protectiveness ripples from him in waves. Maybe it's a play on his name, or maybe he was an ugly child who grew up to be perfect, giving a big *fuck you* to the ones who didn't give him a shot for being different. I find beauty in the different.

Me: What can I call you?

I want to be separated from the ones he calls friends. I want my own special name for him, one just for us.

Unknown: Are we not friends?

Me: I was hoping for more...

Unknown: Next time we meet, I'll tell you so you know what to call me when you whimper my name.

If I wasn't embarrassed before, I surely am now. Images of us naked, rolling around in a bed, cause a low moan to ripple from me. I don't want him to know how inexperienced I am or the effect that text had on me, so I try to play it cool.

Me: Are you watching me?

Unknown: I wish I was. Unfortunately, I'm all alone with just my imagination.

I frown because the flash of white I saw was most definitely a figment of *my* imagination.

Me: Can you imagine me moaning, Master?

Send. *Oh, God.*

Me: Master*

Goddammit.

Me: Monster! Monster! Oh God, autocorrect just killed me.

I want to curl up in a ball and hide in my duvet. My heart hammers like a wild horse trying to be tamed inside my chest.

Unknown: I want to talk to you.

I've just saved his number into my phone when it

rings in my hand. "Monster" flashes across the screen, and I nearly drop it in my haste to pick up.

"Hello?" I squeak out, my voice slightly shaky.

"Hi, Doll." His voice is deep, throaty, raspy. It does things to my insides. Lights them on fire. Turns them upside down. Sends currents of electricity surging through them.

I'm still embarrassed I typed "Doll" when I added my number instead of my name, but I can't help but wonder, based on his comments, if he's the one who gifted me the dolls. I also gave the name Doll because I wasn't exactly ready to tell him my name and liked the idea of hiding under my doll persona. Seemed fitting at the time. Now…I'm not so sure. Makes me feel like a child. He's a lot older than me, and now I wonder if he sees me as this dumb, young girl. Disappointment in myself causes me to shudder.

"Hi, Monster."

We're both quiet for a moment, and I feel awkward. My insecurities are blinking like a neon sign.

"Um, I…" I trail off.

"Call me Master, little doll. I like the sounds of your breathing."

My heart skips a beat. "Your voice sounds deeper on the phone. It's like it rattles through me. Like it's inside me." I want to smack myself for sounding so stupid. A groan of embarrassment escapes me.

"Mmmm, pretty doll," he murmurs. "I like the idea of *me* inside *you*."

I choke on my words as a pulse of warm excitement floods over my body. He's so forward. I've been around Jason, who is also forward, but in a totally different way.

With Monster—er…Master, I want him to say dirty things to me. To kiss and touch me. "I…I don't even know you…" I breathe, my muscles tightening and tingling as foreign sensations dance low in my stomach.

"I think you do," he says in a tone that makes me think he's hinting to the doll. He chuckles, and my body burns with desire. "You're going to know me well—and very soon. That, I can promise you."

I bite my lip. "Are we going to go out on a date?"

"We're going to go on all the dates. I'm going to kiss you again, Doll. I'm going to spend more than three seconds exploring your sweet mouth. I've been craving you since the moment we spoke in the bookstore. I know you feel the same." His tone is so smug. So sure. And he's absolutely correct. *What is this?*

My emotions overflow, rippling through my body like a storm over the ocean. The push and pull is chaotic and uncontrollable. I can't fight it. I won't fight it. I simply don't want to.

"I want that," I murmur, my words once again feeling childish on my tongue.

"I know."

I giggle, some of the tension leaving my body. "You're so sure of yourself."

"I am. Sometimes you just have an overwhelming feeling, Doll. You're that overwhelming feeling. Seeped deep in my pores. Taken hold of my nerve endings. Jolted my lonely spirit back to life." His tone darkens. "I want you like I've never wanted anything in my entire life."

He speaks to me in the same way the heroes in my books do. Alpha males, they call them. Bossy and sure and hot. Domineering. While Elise is dealing with dumb boys, I have a real man on the other line. A man who wants to devour me.

"What if I'm not enough?" I ask him, my voice a mere whisper.

"You're everything," he growls.

I've never been growled at in such a possessive way. It scrambles my brain and has me thinking irrational thoughts.

"I want to see you now," I blurt out, my gaze flitting to the window. Maybe he is outside. Wishful thinking.

Another growl. "Soon. I promise."

I don't understand the overwhelming need surging through me. It consumes me. Violates me. Disturbs me. Teases me.

"When?" Oh God, I sound so needy.

"Tomorrow," he vows.

"Okay." My voice cracks, and I hate it. No wonder I don't do well in the boyfriend department like my sister. I can hardly talk to a potential one on the phone without turning into a psycho.

"Doll," he groans, his voice husky. "Send me a picture of you."

Heat surges through me. "I just took a shower. My hair's a mess. I don't have any makeup on."

He's silent other than his ragged breathing. And for a moment, I fear I've scared him off. "Please." His tone is sad almost. Pleading. Just as needy as how I feel. Emotion he shows just for me. My eyes only.

I swallow. "Okay."

Putting the phone on speaker, I turn it around and

cringe when I see my reflection. My hair is wet and tangled. My face is pale and puffy. But it's then I see my nipple poking through my robe opening. Lining up the camera where it's barely visible, I smile before snapping the pic. It feels naughty, taking a picture of my nipple. I want him to think it's an accident.

Before I can change my mind, I press send, and hear the buzzing on his end.

"I told you I look a mess," I whisper.

Another growl resounds through the line. It reaches deep inside me, owning a part of me I never knew existed. "Put me on that Facetime thing these phones do." His demand is hot and leaves no room for argument. And I don't want to argue. I want to see him. Eagerly, I mash the button, and within seconds, his handsome face is staring back at me.

But he's angry.

Scowling.

Infuriated.

I frown. "You're mad."

He bites down on the inside of his lip, and I can't help but lick mine in response.

"I'm not mad," he assures me, his jaw ticking in an angry way. "Show me the rest."

I play dumb. "W-What?"

His gaze softens, and he smiles. The grin that lights up his face gives him a boyish quality that warms my heart. "I'm like an addict, Doll. You can't give me a little hit and not expect me to crave more. I want to overdose on you. I need it. Get me high, beautiful."

I'm lost in the way he begs for these dirty things from

me. I find myself tugging at the rope on my robe, exposing my chest. I can't, however, find the nerve to show him.

What if he doesn't like what he sees?

What if my breasts are too small?

What if he hangs up?

"Please." Again with the pleading that sets my heart aflame.

Closing my eyes, I drag the phone lower, revealing my breasts. The hitch of his breath tells me he likes what he sees. My own breathing is ragged and uneven.

"More, Doll."

I meet his gaze once again on the screen. Hunger and darkness flicker in his eyes. It turns me on so much, I can hardly stand it. "S-Show me *you*," I challenge, my voice raspy with need. I've heard horror stories of girls doing things like this and being burned, but the look on his face, the need in his voice, the overwhelming ache taking over my entire being, tells me this is more. This is two souls reaching for one another. Like gravity, we are being pulled to each other.

He chuckles. "Are we bargaining?"

I lick my lips and nod. "Yes. It's only fair."

"I show you my cock, and you'll show me your perfect cunt?"

An audible gasp wisps from my lips before I can control it. My words remain lodged in my throat as I regard him in shock. I meant like his bare chest or something. But now that he's offering his cock, I'm curious about it. Is it long? Thick? Veiny? Pierced? We haven't talked about his age, but it's obvious he's much older than me, and with his looks, he's probably been with lots of women. I don't want him to think I'm a naïve little girl. I want him to view me as a sexual being, one capable of keeping up with him.

"Okay," I tell him, nerves dancing around my insides.

A growl. "You're such a good girl, Doll."

His praise washes over me like sunshine. Hot. Brilliant. Invigorating. I want to soak it up and lie beneath him all day long. He tosses the phone down, and I get to stare at the ceiling fan in his room while he shuffles about. Then, I hear the mattress springs squeak. When he grabs the phone again, I get a view of his tattooed chest and neck. Heat floods south, and I let out a small mewl. The tattoo on his neck chases over his shoulder, across his peck, and down the side, talons from the beast digging into the rib area. Is this why they call him Monster? Because of the tattoo of just that—a rabid beast who moves as he does? The brutality mixed with his beauty is a stunning contrast.

"I'm ready," I whisper.

"Good," he utters, "because now that I've started with you, I can't stop."

I can't even process his words. I'm simply lost in this naughty moment with him. When the screen starts lowering down his beautifully carved chest, I can't help but gape. I've never seen a man this sculpted to perfection in real life. He's built like a model. Chiseled and flawless. But there's something dark about him. Like a beautiful criminal model. Something familiar too, as if our souls know each other. I'm still lusting over his abs when I get a glimpse of the root of his cock.

Thick and veiny, just like I'd imagined. The dark hair around it is clipped short. My mouth waters. I know my eyes are wide with wonder. I should fear him, be intimidated maybe, but the power I possess to make him this hard—this wonton and greedy to see me—drives me wild. He's willing to share himself. So vulnerable. So striking. So mine.

"More," I whimper, wanting to see the entire thing.

His face shows back up, and as hot as his bearded face is, I want to see his dick. "Show me your pussy. Is it wet?"

I let out a choked sound. "I don't know."

"Show me." His tone is fierce and demanding.

I yield to his words. Jesus, do I yield to them.

My screen drags down along my body, and when I get to my bare pussy, I hold the camera still. The groans from him make my core throb.

"Are you wet?" he asks again, his voice throaty and hoarse.

"Show me what I want to see," I negotiate, "and I'll show you."

I tilt the screen up so I can see him, and what I see makes me whine. His strong hand has his entire thick cock in his grip. It's hard as stone. The head glistens with pre-cum. He strokes himself slowly, and I find myself fixated on the way the veins in his forearm bulge with the movement.

"You're so big," I whisper.

"Show me your sweet pussy, Doll."

His words are like gasoline on the flames flickering inside me. Dragging the screen lower, I show him as he's requested.

"More. Spread your legs apart and show me how wet you are," he growls. His breathing is noisy as he continues to stroke himself.

I drop my thighs apart, feeling completely self-conscious but also naughty, sexy, womanly—I obey him. I'm about to bring the phone back up so I can see his cock again when he barks out an order.

"Fingers. Inside. Now, Doll."

The way he says the words dizzies me. This is dirty and twisted. I barely know him. Heck, I don't even know his name. Yet, here I am, showing him parts of me no other has seen before, touched before. Sliding my free hand down, I push my finger into my slick opening.

"More. Put more fingers inside my pretty pussy. I want you saturated with need." He's practically snarling his words, losing control. Like the very threads holding him up are snapping. *Pop! Pop! Pop!* I feel empowered knowing I have such control over a man. This man.

I push another finger inside.

"A third," he hisses.

"It's too tight," I whisper. "It burns."

"Put three fingers in your hole, Doll. Do it now. My cock is going to really fucking burn when I push it inside you, so I need you to get yourself good and ready."

I moan at his words. He wants to fuck me. Monster wants to fuck me. I'm buzzing with need and excitement. Losing my virginity to the hottest man I've ever encountered feels like a dream. A fantasy come to life.

Pushing the third finger in, I cry out. It hurts. I don't understand how his giant cock will fit in there.

"Fuck," he grunts. "Goddamn, you're so perfect."

I beam under his praise. "Thank you."

"Take your slippery fingers and touch your clit. I want to hear you moan, Doll, while I look inside your open, quivering hole," he rasps. His voice is broken and desperate. Once again, power surges through me.

Slipping my fingers from my sore sex, I begin massaging my clit. It's difficult to hold the phone in one hand while I masturbate with the other, but I do my best for him. My eyes flutter closed, and I get lost in the moment, imagining him on top of me. Overpowering me. Nipping at my throat as he bucks into me. It doesn't take long before I'm losing my mind to an orgasm only possible because of him. My orgasms never feel this good. They don't grab a hold of my soul by the throat and shake it.

"Master," I cry out, my entire body jolting with pleasure. My pussy contracts, pulsating with my racing heart.

"Let me see your face," he barks out.

I jerk the screen up to where I'm staring at his cock again, staring straight into the tip as he jacks himself off. Soon, he grunts, and his cum spurts against the screen. It's the single most erotic thing I've ever seen in my life.

My eyes flutter closed as he cleans off his phone. Now that I'm sated, I prop the phone against the pillow and curl up on my side. Sleepiness wraps its claws around me, threatening to drag me under.

"You're so beautiful. Sing me a song, Doll."

I sing him one of my favorite nursery rhymes. The one about Miss Polly. My eyes are closed, but I can hear his heavy breathing as it seems to cloud around me, possessing me. He's so intense. I've never known anyone like this before. He's different. Special. Mine.

My eyes blink open at that thought.

He's watching me with soft eyes. The look on his face melts my heart.

"Do you believe in fate?" I ask, a sigh on my lips.

He nods, something akin to sorrow flitting briefly in his eyes. "Fate brought you back to me."

"What do you mean?"

Shaking his head, he smiles. "Fate made us bump into each other at the bookstore."

"Fate knows what she's doing." I yawn.

"Keep your fingers dirty for me, Doll," he murmurs. "But I want you to go to sleep now. You need your rest."

"Why?" I yawn again, barely able to keep my eyes open.

"Because I'm coming for you."

I shiver and blink my eyes open. "You are?"

"I'm coming for you very soon. We're going to be so good together. No running."

The fierceness in his voice indicates something much darker than a simple date or one-night stand. But I read too much into everything. My mind has already conjured the idea that Master and his Doll are boyfriend and girlfriend. I've named our three future children. Already started signing his last name I don't even know in my mind.

"I can't wait," I assure him. Whatever he wants, I'm down for it. Anything to have him stare at me with such possession flickering in his gaze.

"You won't have to for long."

CHAPTER ELEVEN

~ Unique ~

Benny

"G ET DRESSED," TANNER BARKS. "WE'RE leaving in ten."

I rub sleep out of my eyes and grit my teeth. My plan was to get up and figure out a way to see Bethany. I'm irritated Tanner has me going on some bullshit errand at the crack of dawn before I've even gotten a chance to speak to her.

As I take a quick shower and brush my teeth, I can't help but remember all the soft, pale curves of her body. I've never seen anything so beautiful before. I'd lost my mind a little last night. I demanded things of her before I could even get control of myself.

But my pretty new doll obeyed my commands.

She showed me her perfect flesh and made herself come.

I never expected her to be so pliable. It's as though she were made just for me—a match that's finally been brought together.

I'm fucking obsessed with her.

I dress in some dark, holey jeans and a tight black

Metallica shirt before stuffing my feet in some boots. Once I leave my room, I find Tanner leaning against the wall by the door, two Starbucks coffees in his hands. His amber eyes are calm and relaxed. The tension I've felt from him lately has lessened.

It pisses me off.

The dynamic between Tanner and I has shifted. Kami is at fault, I just know it. If I could figure out how to slit her throat and hide the body without Tanner finding out, I would. I still may. I'm going to think about it.

We're silent as we walk out to his black Escalade. He drives for a good ten minutes before speaking.

"I take it the errand went well," he says, his eyes remaining on the road.

So much has happened between then and now, it takes a moment for my mind to catch up. "Yep. Bitch screamed like a stuck pig when I sawed off her tongue." I stare out the side window so he doesn't see the lie written on my face.

"Hmmm. And the other guy was just a casualty?"

"Eliminate witnesses. First rule of Tanner Club."

He snorts, and I smile.

"I have a gift for you, Benjamin. Something you've worked hard to deserve," he says, pride in his tone.

My shoulders relax, and I lean against the leather. "If it's another doll, I'm not interested."

"Better," he assures me. "Much better."

We drive and drive. I lose track of time, but we're at least an hour outside town when he turns down a dirt road lined with thick trees on either side. Nerves light up inside me.

Is he taking me out here to kill me?

He can fucking try. Others have tried and failed.

Nah, if Tanner wanted me dead, he'd have tried to slit my throat in my bed while I slept and had his cleaners take care of my body.

The dirt road goes on for quite some time. Anticipation builds inside me. I'm buzzing and can't tell whether it's the coffee, what's to come, or both. We eventually pull up to a mobile home. It's ratty and old. Disappointment trickles through me. I'd expected something nicer.

"Don't pout, Benjamin. That isn't your surprise."

I grit my teeth, but nod. He parks the Escalade and climbs out. In his suit, he looks out of place against the woodsy backdrop. I follow him around the trailer to the backside. When I see a concrete elevated surface with a door built in, my excitement thunders through me once again.

"What is it?" I question.

He tosses me a key on a skull keychain. "Check it out, Monster. It's all yours." His grin is wolfish, but I don't miss the small flicker of uncertainty in his eyes. He wants me to like whatever it is. I already do.

Unlocking the padlock, I unhook it from the door, tossing it into the grass, and wrench open the rusty door. It creaks in protest, and I'm impressed to find stairs rather than a ladder descending into the earth.

"What in the fuck is this?" I marvel aloud.

"A bunker. I purchased this property from a guy who was certain the apocalypse was coming. The old man was prepared as fuck," he tells me. *Like my dad was.* "He died, and now, it's mine. Yours. It's my gift to you."

I grin at him over my shoulder before trotting down the steps that go at least twenty feet into the earth. He follows behind me, flipping a switch on the wall. The bunker lights up, and as soon as I'm inside, I'm blown away. It's not some storm shelter or a place to store crap. It's a home. Someone had plans to live down here if shit hit the fan. It's built out into rooms. An actual living room and kitchen are what I come to first. Sofa. Recliner. Refrigerator. Table. The works. Like a kid on Christmas, I explore the giant space. Canned goods, water, and other supplies line the shelves at every turn. I discover a bedroom with a double bed. The room is spacious, and my dick twitches as I consider Bethany sprawled out naked on the quilt.

"I love it," I growl. "It's so fucking awesome."

"We haven't even gotten to the best part," he tells me. "This way."

He shuffles past me, then strides down a long corridor. At the end, he pushes through a door. When I step inside behind him, I grin. It isn't exactly the way I would have done it, but it certainly works. Side by side are three sturdy cells, much like the ones he was fucking Kami in. They're made of Plexiglas or something—thick and seemingly impenetrable. Each cell is fitted with a heavy padlock and small circles are cut in the top for air circulation. Inside each is a folded blanket, a dog bowl, and a bucket to piss in. The room around the cells is tiled from floor to ceiling and the halogen light flickers and hums. In the center of the large room is a drain. If things get messy, a quick hose down would be all it would take to clean it up.

"What do you think?" he asks, a wide grin on his face. "This is the part I had done up just for you."

I want to ask if he thinks he'll like *his* cell, but I don't. One day, when he's tucked safely inside and I'm disemboweling Kami in front of him, I will ask then.

"It's perfect. I'm going to get her now," I tell him as I start past him.

He grabs my bicep and shakes his head. "Slow down, killer. You can't simply accost the girl. We need a plan. That isn't the plan."

"I do have a plan," I snap. "I'm going to take her out on a date. Then, I'll bring her back here. She'll come willingly. Bethany wants me."

His amber eyes narrow as he studies me. "Since when?"

I freeze and clench my jaw. "Maybe if you weren't so busy with Kami, I would have had an opportunity to tell you."

Our eyes meet in a heated challenge.

"Tell me what I missed." His tone is soft but cold.

"I kissed her. Ran into her and kissed her." A smile tugs at my lips. I don't tell him we had phone sex or that I was stalking her at the bookstore. I don't tell him about her doll gift, or the fact that I sense she knows it's from me. I certainly don't tell him I almost got my ass caught by Dillon Fucking Scott.

"Odd."

I lift a brow. "Why is that so odd?"

"Seems vague is all."

Meeting his stare, I look him dead in the eye. "I ran into her yesterday. When she looked up, there was attraction there. I asked her if I could walk her home. She felt the connection, Tanner. I saw it in her eyes. So, I walked her home, kissed her pretty mouth, and got her number."

His mouth twitches into a smile. "How adorable."

I give him a shove. "Fuck off. She's different. The moment was intense."

"I bet it was."

Ignoring him, I continue to prowl the space and explore. It's so fucking perfect, I can't even deal.

He eventually leaves the bunker, and I take the time to call Bethany.

"Hello?" Her tone is soft and sexy as fuck.

"Morning, beautiful."

She sighs, and the sound rustles my cock awake. "Morning. I didn't expect a wake-up call." There's a smile in her voice—a smile I want to kiss away.

"You're going to hear my voice every morning," I tell her. Soon, I'll wake her up with my dick deep inside her and my teeth scraping along her throat.

She chuckles, and it makes me wonder how it would feel with my cock stuffed down her throat. Would it vibrate? Could I come from her sweet laughter?

"My mom is gone for three days at a seminar that just came up. We had to cancel our pedicures and everything. Anyway, Elise always goes out on Friday nights. I thought…" she trails off, her voice becoming unsure. "I thought maybe you could come over. I'm a good cook. I could make you dinner and…"

I could feed my cock to you for dessert.

"Yeah?" My voice is husky with need.

"We could see what happens after that. Watch a movie or—"

"Fuck?"

She squeaks. "Master."

"Yes, my pretty doll?"

A sigh.

Her sighs speak straight to my cock.

"I'm a virgin. I'm not sure if…I mean…I want to…"

I thought she was, but hearing her confirm she's saved herself for me is music to my ears. She waited and will only ever know my cock and my love. It fucking does things to me.

"Go slow?" I almost choke.

Over my goddamn dead body.

"Maybe."

She can't even say the word without lying. My doll wants this as much as I do. She wants me to take her and keep her. To fuck her and love her.

"I'll do my best," I lie. "And I haven't had a home-cooked meal in ages." Not a lie. "Mostly, I just want to see you." Truth.

"I want to see you too. Seven okay?" she asks. "I wanted to have enough time to go buy something pretty to wear."

I don't want her to wear anything new. I want her to wear something she's made.

"I'm sure you have something lovely in your closet. Don't buy anything. Surprise me with something simple. My favorite color is white." Pure, like snow. Untouched, like my Bethany's virgin cunt. And when her innocence drips from her lips between her thighs, we'll ruin the perfect dress, and it will be beautiful.

"Are you sure?"

"Absolutely," I assure her. "It's coming off anyway."

"Master!" she cries out, then laughs. "Slow. Remember?"

Oh, I remember, I just don't give a fuck.

"Of course, Doll."

We eventually hang up, and I find Tanner watching me, his brows lifted in surprise.

"Will you require my assistance in getting her here?" he asks.

I flash him a crooked grin. "No, but I do need some rope. Can you get that for me?"

"I thought you were going to lure her here? She wants you, right?" he challenges.

"I need the rope to *keep* her here. In my bed. My sweet Bethany isn't going anywhere."

He laughs, and it sounds devilish. "There's my Monster. I'll get you your rope."

The day drags on and on. To pass the time, once Tanner dropped me back off, I walked down to a postal box and sent my father a nice *fuck you* letter with a picture of my new doll as a bonus, just to taunt the old cunt, knowing I have her and there's nothing he can do about it. It's funny how karma comes back around.

I wander into an old antique shop near the club, finding all kinds of bullshit. The store is dead aside from someone rummaging around in the back. Old trinkets. Ancient furniture. Dusty books. In the back corner, I discover an aging vanity. Small, like it's designed for a girl. Perfect for my doll to put her doll on. The mirror is still intact, the edges are carved ornately, and it has a single drawer beneath it, but it's well over my budget. I could probably ask Tanner for the money, but then he'd know I was buying a gift for my pretty new doll. I'll have to sort this one out on my own. I'm still admiring the piece when an old woman hollers at me from a ladder.

"Need some help, young man?"

"How firm are you on this vanity? I don't have three hundred bucks," I admit.

She straightens some books on the shelf and swipes the dust off them with her rag. "I'm in the business to make money, not give it away."

Yeah, bitch, well I'm in the business of making sure I have enough money to keep my pretty new doll, not spending it on your overpriced attitude.

I grit my teeth. "I'll give you two. That's all I have on me."

Lies. But she'll be lucky if she gets that.

"Three." She stuffs the rag into her belt. "If you can't afford this store, please run along to the Walmart."

Her snippy attitude bothers me. Approaching the ladder, I glare up at her.

"Two."

She jerks her head down and frowns, her wrinkly lips pressing together. "Three."

Stubborn old bitch.

I grip the base of the ladder. "Two."

"Three—ahhh!"

In a single moment of fury at this dumb bat's attitude, I jerk the ladder hard. Losing her footing, she crashes to the concrete floor, her head hitting the surface with a loud pop. I stare in fascination as blood pools around her. It never gets old.

I shake away my daze. Well…fuck. I didn't mean to do that. Snatching the dust rag from her belt, I wipe off the ladder where I touched it, then tuck it into my pocket. I heft the vanity into my grip and slip out the back of the building. It takes longer going behind the buildings because I have to wedge the vanity past dumpsters and shit, but eventually, I get it home. Later, I'll take it to its permanent home.

For a moment, I worry about drawing the police so close to The Vault, but figure they'll see it as an accident. The old antique store didn't even have a computer cash register. Everything was old, I'm certain they didn't have security cameras. The old lady fell from the ladder and cracked her head open. Open and shut case. They won't suspect a thing.

Me: I'm starved.

Doll: For me or my famous spaghetti?

Me: Does it make me an asshole if I say both?

Doll: Actually, it's sweet that you want me to cook for you.

Me: Nothing sweet is running through my head right now. Is it seven yet?

Doll: So impatient. I'm shopping for the ingredients as we speak.

I want to tell her I know this because I'm two aisles over following her, but I refrain.

Me: I bought you a gift.

I hear a squeal of excitement across the grocery store,

and it makes me smile like a fucking idiot.

Doll: Really?! That's so sweet. What is it?
Me: It's a surprise.
Doll: I hate surprises.

I can almost imagine her lips pouting. Soon, I'll have those lips wrapped around my cock. She will learn to love surprises…I have a few.

Me: You'll love this one.

Peeking around the corner, I'm delighted to see her staring at her phone, her cheeks brilliant red. The dress she's wearing for me is white and lacy. Innocent, but short. The knee-highs are sexy as fuck. She looks like a little girl in a woman's body. My cock is painfully hard in my jeans.

Doll: What do you think about chocolate cake? Mine is to die for.
Me: My mouth is watering…
Doll: Bad Master.

She's smiling as she starts pushing her cart toward the baking aisle. I peer down that aisle as a tall, lanky motherfucker calls out her name.

"Elizabeth? Is that you? I almost didn't recognize you. Holy fuck, that outfit is hot," he groans. He runs his fingers through his blond hair and flashes her a flirty smile. He's not alone. A couple other guys waggle their eyebrows behind him before carrying a case of beer to the counter, shouting they'll see him back at Randy's.

A possessive growl rumbles from my throat.

"Jason," she bites out in a cool tone as she pulls down a can of condensed milk. "Good seeing you, but I'm in a hurry. I have a date."

My chest tightens at her words, but the motherfucker

isn't deterred.

"I could keep you company until your date. I was bummed you didn't stay for the movie last night," he says, his tone fake sad. The dumbass kid is sporting a weak boner in his jeans. A boner for *my* doll.

"Not interested," she snips. "Now, if you'll excuse me." She starts past him, but he grips her elbow hard enough to make her yelp.

My teeth clench, and I fist my phone so hard, I'm afraid it might crack. I want to go pry him away from her, but I can't interfere where I know there are cameras. The ball cap on my head hides my appearance now, but if I slaughter that stupid fuck in the baking aisle, it might raise some suspicion.

"We could hang out in my car after this. You. Me. This dress," he mumbles as he lifts the back of it.

This dipshit needs to die. I start down the aisle, no longer worried about getting caught, when I hear a sick crack.

Jason grunts and stumbles away as she hurries down the aisle away from him. When our eyes meet, he stares at me in confusion as he swipes blood away from his forehead. The condensed milk can she had rolls at his feet.

My sweet, feisty doll just kicked this fucker's ass.

I've never been so proud in my life.

With a smirk, I abandon him and slip out past where she is checking out. Once I'm settled in my car, I watch as she walks out with two sacks in her arms. I want to follow after her so fucking badly. To make sure she gets home safely. I mean, fuck, that dress is going to stop traffic or get her kidnapped or some shit, and no one is taking my doll—no one but me.

But I have more pressing matters to attend to.

My cock jolts.

I ignore that matter as well.

Turning my gaze back to the store, I wait for Jason to emerge. Strolling to his shiny red Mustang, he climbs in, and I follow him all the way to an apartment. He's oblivious to the world around him as he attempts to stop the bleeding on his head.

Oh, son, you're going to bleed a fuck lot more than that for touching my doll.

I stalk behind him as he takes the stairs and unlocks the door to an apartment, slipping through before the door can close behind him. The fucker is in such a hurry to get to the bathroom, he doesn't even notice me following after him. I'm cautious in case this isn't his apartment and others are inside, but it's silent until I hear him cursing. Then, the shower starts. I slip into a bedroom and sit at the desk. With a quick move of the mouse, the computer wakes back up, and what I see pisses me right the fuck off.

Her.

My Bethany.

Pictures.

So many pictures.

This has to be his apartment.

Most are of her and Elise, probably stolen from Facebook, but others are ones he took of her without her noticing. In the dark at the movies. Her watching the screen with a scowl on her face. Pictures of his hand on her thigh. So many dark, grainy pictures of her thighs. Motherfucker.

I delete them all. I don't want him having pictures of her for others to see when they're combing through his belongings. Once I'm sure she's deleted from his life, I storm into his bathroom. The shower curtain is slightly agape, and the loser is jacking off his mediocre cock, no doubt remembering Bethany in her pretty dress. Fury surges through me.

"She's mine," I snarl as I snag the curtain open.

The fucker's eyes are wide as he screeches in surprise. Grabbing him by his jaw, I yank him out of the shower, and he slips, but my brutal hold prevents him from busting his ass.

"You think you can touch what's mine and not get punished?" I hiss, careful to keep my voice down, knowing neighbors are everywhere.

"N-No. I have n-no idea wh-what you're t-talking about," he sputters.

I knee him in the balls, and he cries like a little bitch, then yelps when I shove him into his room.

"Put your goddamn clothes on before I skin your cock and staple it to your forehead."

"Y-You're not g-going to rape and kill me?" he asks in astonishment.

Freak.

"Rape you?" I howl, laughing. "In your dreams, stupid fuck."

He glowers at me, and it pisses me off.

"Unless that's what you want, pretty boy," I snarl as I pounce on him. He struggles, but I manage to pin him face down. "Want the big scary man's dick in your ass?"

He sobs, his body shuddering beneath me. "N-No. P-Please."

I laugh, cold and dark. "I'm not gay, asshole. I'm in love with the woman you thought you could touch."

"Elizabeth? You're her boyfriend?"

"I'm her master."

"I'm sorry," he chokes out. "She never mentioned you."

My phone buzzes with a phone call, and I yank a shirt from the floor, then cram it in his mouth as I straddle him. Once I'm sure he'll be quiet, I answer the phone.

"Bad news," Bethany says in a sad tone. "I dropped my bag with the eggs. Looks like the chocolate cake isn't going to happen." She sounds positively distraught over that fact.

"Make it for me some other time, Doll. I'll get *your* dessert later, right?"

She laughs, seeming to relax. "I thought I said go slow."

"I'll eat my dessert *really* slow, beautiful. So slow, you'll beg me to go faster."

Her breath hitches. "You may be too much for me."

"And I'll never get enough of you."

Dumb fuck struggles and grunts beneath me, so I use my elbow to give him a whack to the temple, knocking his ass out without leaving a bruise.

"See you in two hours," she says, her voice happy. "We'll just see where the night takes us." The night is going to take us straight to my bunker where I'll spend the night fucking her into oblivion.

"See you soon, Doll."

We hang up, and I hustle. I have just enough time to take care of this motherfucker and get back to my doll.

I quickly type up a note on his computer: **I'm sorry, but I just can't do this anymore.**

Once that's done and I've swiped my prints from the keyboard, I drag him to the window. With a hasty glance, I make sure this second story apartment is up high enough, then shove him head first past the frame. His body lands with a satisfying thwack.

I'm coming for you, pretty new doll…

CHAPTER TWELVE

~ Pure ~

Dillon

"Same guy?" Marcus asks, looking down at the dead guy with a two-inch gash in his throat. We're back at Rebel's Reds where we got the call about a homicide in the early hours of the morning. I'm still pissed this place reopened so soon. Apparently, Mr. Law didn't own the building. He just managed the club, and his trafficking dealings weren't run through the business accounts. So, legally, we couldn't prevent the owner from moving a new manager in and keeping the place as is.

Un-fucking-believable.

It's now seven a.m. and we're left with a crime scene that, according to the estimated time of death, is around ten hours stale. "Coincidence?" Marcus adds.

I don't believe in coincidences in our line of work. This place was going to be my first stop today to question Scarlet, the eyewitness who placed Harris here on the day of Law's murder. I didn't expect to be here for another homicide. This one is different. One cut, quick kill, no other injuries. There are boot prints in the pool of blood around his head, which is either the person who found him or the killer.

If it is the killer, there is no way it's the same guy who committed Law's murder. He wouldn't have been so careful at one scene only to be so reckless at another.

"I already know what you're thinking, but maybe this guy was an accident. Maybe he was here for someone else, or works here and this guy found out or threatened him?" Marcus spouts out theories.

"I want the trash combed through in case the killer dumped the murder weapon," I bark my orders. "I want everything there is to know about the vic, and no one leaves until we have all statements from employees. I want a list of all employees working last night."

My eyes never leave the body as I search and analyze every inch of him and the scene around him. Getting a first look is so important. Crime scenes are so easily disrupted, and something small overlooked in the start of the investigation can be a game changer when it comes to finding the clues leading us to the suspect. Just to the right of the victim is a small pooling of blood with some drips around it. The drips don't lead up to where the victim fell. "Marcus," I call, distracting him from talking to one of the employees.

I point to the separated blood. His steely grey eyes scan the small puddle of blood and the pattern of the spray.

"Second vic?" he murmurs, speaking my thoughts aloud as a startled screech sounds out from behind us. The lid from one of the dumpsters slams shut and a pale looking Josey holds a hand over her mouth, shaking her head. She's a family friend of Marcus's and is in training to be a detective. Marcus insisted she come with us, but warned her not to touch anything. Like she would listen. This is the third time she's come out with us, and the fucking last, if I have anything to do with it.

She continues to shake her head, pointing at the dumpster.

It's clear she's not going to be able to speak, so with a huff, Marcus moves to the dumpster and flips the lid.

"Shit," he grumbles, stepping away. He leans his nose into the crook of his arm as if to block out a smell. My partner wears suits like he's a character on *Mad Men* or some shit, but right now, he doesn't look so put together as he all but scrambles from the dumpster.

Taking the few steps and a deep breath, I prepare myself for what could be in there. Flies hover and hum, and mixed between the trash bags and leftover food people have chucked in there is a red-haired female.

Scarlet.

Fuck.

Twenty-three years old. Her tongue cut out of her head, and taken as...what? A souvenir? These were personal killings, connected by the club, which points to business rivalry or inside hostility.

Why take her tongue?

She spoke to us and gave us Cassian.

Was this him seeking revenge?

Shutting up witnesses?

How would he know she spoke to us?

A steaming cup is placed in front of me, and it's only then I remember the precinct is full and I've been lost in thought at my desk. Josey smiles at me from where she's taken a seat on the other side of my desk.

"So, any leads?" she asks, and my brow furrows.

Like I'd share that information with her.

She's feisty, but young and naïve. That doesn't always bode well for a female detective. "I brought you coffee," she says, eyeballing the cup I watched her place there moments before.

"What? Do you want a tip?" I retort, reaching for a nickel from the pot I keep on my desk and flicking it to her.

"Don't throw money at me," she snaps. "I'm not a stripper." She tries to sound affronted, but there's a challenge in her tone.

"Are you saying you'd only get nickels tossed at you if you were?" I snort, and her face blanches, turning eight shades of humiliated. She needs a tougher skin to work in a mostly male-dominated career. Before Jade, before MJ, I would have just let her suck it up and learn. Just because she's female doesn't make her exempt from the same shit we give every other newbie around here.

The slight tremor in her jaw as she tries to keep her composure has me feeling like an asshole, though. If Jade were here, I know for a fact she would have punched me straight in the junk for not going easy on her.

"Josey, I'm just yanking your chain. Thank you for the coffee, but I can't divulge any information to you. Now, if you want to be helpful, you can type some of this shit up for me."

I hand her some paperwork, and a small smile creeps over her face.

Perfect. Now she's going to hang around me like a bad smell.

Newbies always have too much enthusiasm for me. I like my colleagues broken in, quiet, and there for a non-vocal drink and conversation after a tough day if I ever need it.

The humming of the overhead air conditioner is driving me crazy, and my stomach is grumbling, begging me to feed it. I get up and round my desk, but my feet halt when my very pregnant wife walks through the doors. She's dressed in a pantsuit, and if you didn't know to look for it, you wouldn't notice the bump hidden beneath her jacket. Her skin is glowing, and she's gained the perfect amount of weight that makes her ass bounce as she walks. Fuck, she makes me hard every damn time, even if it's only been hours since I saw her last. People greet her with affection and respect. She's been missed around here. There was a time when she wouldn't leave this place, and I used to ridicule her for practically living here.

"Pregnancy suits her," Josey says breathlessly from behind me.

Why the fuck has she left her chair just to gawk at my wife?

I look over my shoulder at her to see her watching longingly as Jade talks to Detective Roberts about MJ starting a creative movement class for toddlers next week. It'll be good for when they're ready to start martial arts, as Jade insists. I think she's a little too young, but Jade doesn't, and I don't argue with the mama bear. I tried once and suffered through blue balls for a week because she sex-starved me. It was torture.

"She looks like Gal Gadot," Josey pipes up again.

"Who?" I mutter.

Josey slaps me on the arm, forcing me to look down at her. Her mouth's agape and she's squinting. *What the fuck?*

"Wonder Woman? God, what year you living in old man?" she grumbles.

"It's not the year I'm living in, wiseass, it's reality. The only superheroes who matter are the ones working their asses off here catching bad guys."

Rolling her eyes, she snorts at me.

"Hey, babe." Jade grins as she approaches. I open my arms and drag her into them.

"I didn't expect to see you here today," I growl into her ear, nibbling just below it, making her body soften and curl further into me. She pulls away and slaps me playfully, her eyes flicking to Josey still standing next to me, invading our space like a fucking creeper.

"Hey." Jade smiles at her, and Josey almost melts into a puddle at her feet.

What the actual hell? Josey has a hard-on for my wife?

"You remember Marcus's Josey?" I grunt.

Josey steps forward and hugs an unsuspecting Jade, whose arms go up, then back down awkwardly.

"Of course," she mutters, giving me a wide eyed *"Who?"* look over Josey's shoulder.

"I'm not Marcus's Josey, by the way. I'm just Josey. Single," Josey flusters.

Giving her a narrowed glare, I hook Jade's arm and march her to an office, calling over my shoulder. "Well, she's Dillon's Jade. Married."

I close the office door and glare through the glass once more at Josey, who smirks at me and goes back to doing my paperwork.

"I came in for a reason," Jade tells me, rummaging through a purse I'm still not used to seeing her carry. Before having MJ, she hated having purses, but being a mom, she's always filling them with baby wipes, pacifiers, and snacks—even when she doesn't have MJ with her.

"This," she sighs, worrying her lip with her top teeth.

I unfold the piece of paper and frown. It's the web address Elise gave me a while back, but I haven't had time to look into it.

"I knew something was off with her, Dillon."

My brows furrow. "What is it?" I'm not sure I want to actually find out.

"It's a fetish site."

Oh God. The last thing I need to see is a girl I still remember in pigtails and braces showing flesh or what the fuck ever on a kink site.

"It's worse than you're thinking." Jade's eyes lower to the floor.

I fucking doubt it.

"Go on," I urge, irritation making my tone gritty. "Just tell me because I sure as fuck am not going to look."

Sighing, Jade pulls out a chair and sits in it. Her hands dust off imaginary lint on her pant legs.

"Jade, for fuck's sake, woman."

Her eyes lift to mine, and terror flickers in them. "Dolls, Dillon."

The word *dolls* causes my blood to chill. My hands

tighten into fists.

"What?"

She bites on her lip as she frowns. "She dresses up as a doll."

Motherfucker.

Fuck.

Jesus Christ.

Goddammit.

"She doesn't do sexual acts. Just acts out being a doll." Her voice quivers. "It's creepy and so like—"

"Don't say his name," I bark.

She fidgets in the chair.

"I'll have a word with her," I assure her as I rub the tension from my neck. "I'll see where this shit is coming from."

She places her hand over mine. "There's someone who comments on there. Dollkeeper is the user name."

"And?"

"He mentions her 'brother' like he knows who she is, and, more importantly, who her brother is. He glamorizes the crimes, Ben—"

"Don't say his name," I interrupt, my tone warning. "It doesn't deserve to ever grace your lips, baby."

She wraps her free arm over her stomach. "I worry that if he has found out who she is, then he could find out where she lives and things could escalate. I printed off all his comments. It's bordering on obsession the way he comments on all her pictures and stuff."

I stroke my hand down her cheek, pushing her hair behind her ear. "I'll go over what you've shown me."

"Even from the grave, that bastard still lingers," she

exhales, a mix of fury and fear in her voice.

No matter how much we move on, he will always linger. Like a motherfucking virus waiting until your immune system is down to strike.

Jade left to go take MJ to see my niece, Jasmine, over an hour ago, and took my appetite with her. I still can't bring myself to log on to the website, so I skip that step and go directly to the source.

"D," Marcus shouts, making me slosh my cold cup of coffee down my shirt. Perfect. He strides toward me, a look of determination on his hard face. The scruff is growing out on his face, making him a little more rugged than usual. I want to give him shit because he's normally a pretty boy, but I know he's going through hell right now. I bite my tongue just this once. "So, I had an idea."

"Congratulations," I grumble, swiping at some tissues and dabbing the brown stain spreading like wildfire over the material of my white shirt.

Rolling his eyes, he hands me the statement taken from Scarlet, aka Jinan Anderson.

"She said the owner of The Vault was the one who interviewed her for the job, which, after meeting him, seemed well out of the ordinary. That stuff is usually done by a bar manager."

"Agreed. What's your point?"

He hands me another piece of paper.

"What's this?"

"It's an application form," he says with a grin.

I raise a brow, waiting for him to elaborate.

"It's for The Vault. I say we send someone in. An unknown to get the low down."

He casts his eyes over to Josey, who's picking dirt out of her nails with a safety pin.

"Fuck no."

"Come on. It's a perfect plan."

"No."

"D." He attempts his heartbreaker puppy dog eyes that work on chicks, but he should know me better than that. I don't fall for his stupid-ass tactics.

"She's not even a detective," I bark.

"Exactly. It's perfect."

My desk phone rings, and Marcus leans over to pick up the receiver. "Okay. Yep. No. Wait for us," he tells the caller, then hangs up the line. His attention turns to me. "A body downtown. A kid either fell, jumped, or was pushed from a second story window."

"And?"

"And Mills said you'll want to be there."

What the fuck does that mean?

"Fine, but you're staying put with Josey. I don't need her poking around another crime scene. And, Marcus," I bark, "don't you two be getting any more non-bright ideas until I'm back."

CHAPTER THIRTEEN

~ Novel ~

Elizabeth

A SMILE TILTS MY LIPS at the aromas filling the air. I place the lid over the pot and give the salad one last toss. Getting ready took me ages. Even though Master didn't want me going to any trouble, I felt the need to embrace who I am…what he calls me. I put on my best doll makeup and a pretty dress—white, matching the panties I'm wearing. My socks cover my knees, and the plain Mary Jane's glisten from their polish.

My feet carry me back to the new gift that was waiting for me on the porch when I returned from shopping. Another precious doll. Although, none are as incredible as the first one he gave me. It's my favorite. My stomach somersaults at the thought of asking Master if he is indeed the one who writes to me under the username Dollkeeper and sends me the gifts. It makes the most sense—the reason things moved so quickly from meeting. Really, this had been building for a while. But then that means he did seek me out. Searched and found me. Imbedded himself into my life. A thrill of appreciation shoots through me.

A text alerts from my cell on the counter, gaining my attention.

Master: I'll be there soon. Be ready.

My heart skips, and I check myself once more in the mirror. The door handle twists open, and my excitement is palpable in the air around me. As the wood door swings open, my heart sinks. Elise waltzes in, accompanied by friends—lots of them. She looks me up and down, then grabs my elbow before marching me into the back room out of view from the people still piling into the house.

Releasing me, she glares up and down my body once more. "This has to stop! Look at you. You look like a porn child," she screeches.

What the hell is a porn child?

"I'm a doll," I clarify.

"No, Beth, you're a person—a damaged one after finding out about our sick, twisted brother and his doll fetish."

"This isn't about that," I lie. In truth, that is exactly where this deep-rooted fixation started.

"Do you have no respect for the people he killed? The women he stole? Jade, for Christ's sake?" she hollers, and shame shrouds me.

This isn't like that. They didn't have a choice. This isn't for our dead brother. This…this is for me.

And Master.

"Why are you even here? Shouldn't you be at the dorms?" I snap, irritation stealing away the high from moments before.

She flinches at the force of my tone. "You know I'm trying to avoid the guy I was seeing. He will go there looking for me, I just need some time."

"Well, you could have asked," I sass. She's going to ruin everything, like usual.

"This is my home too," she argues. "I just like staying at the dorms. And, as a matter of fact, I did ask Mom."

Of course perfect little Elise asked Mom.

"Who are all those people?"

"I'm having a little party. Mom won't be home until Sunday. She said it was fine. I need this, Beth. Don't be a brat."

Me? I need to not be the brat? I want to scream at her at the top of my lungs.

"And, Beth," she calls, stopping at the doorway, "Jason is invited, so play nice."

"Screw you, Elise," I screech, anger, frustration, and hurt colliding inside me. How can my own sister push the subject of stupid, ugly, wandering hands Jason Dickface so hard?

Her mouth hangs open like a blow-up doll waiting for some old weirdo's dick. A snigger slips from my lips at the thought, and I rush past her to grab my cell. I need to beg Master to take me away from here. From her. From everyone.

When the front door opens again and Dillon stands there looking grim, my heart sinks, my stomach knotting at the thought of what must have caused the expression on his usually perfect face.

"What is it?" I breathe, expecting bad news—waiting for it.

He frowns and closes the door, his eyes skirting over to the now bustling kitchen. "You having a dinner party?"

My special dinner. Ruined. *Fucking Elise.*

Elise shakes her head no and ushers him into the back room. I follow behind them and close the door. "What is it, D? You're scaring me."

"I just came from downtown," he utters, his voice strained. "We believe a suicide."

Oh God. Who? Why are you here, dammit?

"I'm sorry, Elise," he says. "It's a kid I've seen you running around with before. Jason Bronson."

Her gasp echoes in the silence. Dillon looks over to me, but I don't have anything to offer him. I hated Jason. I didn't wish death on him, but I don't feel differently about him because he's dead. I'm numb to the news. I feel nothing.

"Why?" she questions, shock shaking her voice.

"Who knows, sweetheart. It's usually a multitude of things that could have easily been remedied if the person had gotten the help they clearly needed. No one is to blame here," he states, his eyes focusing on me, pinning me to the spot I'm standing in.

"Is that all?" I ask, desperate to leave so I can call Master.

"Elizabeth," Elise wheezes, her tear-ridden eyes judging me.

"He was your friend, not mine," I inform her.

"You're so heartless! Who are you?" she yells, coming at me with her hand splayed. The hit happens quick, stinging like flames across my cheek, sending my face jerking sharply to the side from the impact.

Bitch!

Rage roars inside my head like a violently hungry

lion, begging me to break loose and tear her throat out. I'm tired of her—so fucking tired. My temper flares to uncontainable intensity and the urge to yank her stupid fake hair out consumes me, but Dillon encases her in his broad arms before I can react. Snuffs my blazing plans with one simple action of protection. He thinks he's protecting me from *her*. Truth is, though, she needs protection from *me*.

"Look at her," Elise screams, disgust in her tone. "This creepy doll thing. It's out of hand. Someone was taking photos of me the other day, and it's because they think I'm this…*this*…"

"This what?" I shout back at her spoiled outburst.

"This killer loving doll freak," she spits at me.

"That's enough," Dillon barks, and she stops squirming in his hold as she cries into his chest. *Who's the brat, really?*

"I want to talk to you, Beth—about all of this. But not tonight. I think maybe one of you should come home with me to give the other space for the evening."

I'm nineteen years old for God's sake, and as much as I appreciate him looking out for me—for us—he isn't our father.

"No," I state, bitterness in my tone. I have somewhere I can go. Grabbing my cell, I bolt up the stairs.

CHAPTER FOURTEEN

~ Newfangled ~

Benny

Parking the car a few blocks over, I walk toward her house. I'm just stepping into the road to cross over when I see a group of people walking up the path and going inside.

What the fuck?

She didn't say anything about there being more than just her and I.

I send her a text, but get no reply. Rage burns up my spine.

Is she playing me? No, she wouldn't.

Honk-honk!

Light floods up my legs and blinds me as the loud blaring of the horn almost deafens me. Holding my hand up to cover my eyes from the intrusion of light, I step out of the road so the car can pass, and take cover next to a tall tree. My eyes remain on the house, watching, hoping she replies so I don't have to go over and make a scene. The car that almost ran me down pulls over in front of the house, and it's then I recognize who it belongs to.

Fucking Dillon.

What the hell is it with him nearly finding out about me still owning my heartbeat?

Exasperation washes over me. Why is he here? Does he have a hard-on for another one of my dolls? Why haven't I killed that motherfucking slimy prick yet?

He's not there long, and soon, leaves alone. The bedroom light to my doll's room flicks on, and she comes to the window, pushing it wide open and inhaling. She holds her hand to her ear and my cell lights up with her number a second later.

"Doll?" I breathe.

"Master, my sister ruined everything. I hate her. I hate it here. I'm sorry, but can I come to you?" She sniffles, and my soul aches to hold her. Where the hell can I take her that will be discreet and safe? Tanner's surprise flickers into my mind, and I sigh. "I'm waiting for you. Pack a bag. Come outside and walk up two blocks. You will see a black Mustang waiting. Keep your head down," I instruct.

My body hums in anticipation. I can hardly keep still as I wait for her. When I see her running down the street, not being fucking discreet at all with her backpack dangling from her grip, I have the urge to snag her up and stuff her in the backseat so she doesn't cause a scene. But the moment I see her face, highlighted by my headlights, my chest aches. Her pretty makeup is ruined. Black mascara streaks down her rosy cheeks, her nose is bright red, and her juicy pink lips are parted as she sobs. Her white dress bounces as she runs, revealing her milky thighs above her knee-highs. She has tiny tits, but even those are alluring as fuck as she runs.

Run, run, run, Doll, right into my waiting arms.

As soon as she nears, she crashes into me, her tiny body nearly knocking me over. I've never been met with such need and overwhelming emotion. My heart hammers in my chest as I gather her slight form into my arms. I kiss the top of her head and inhale her sweet scent. Much like a child, she cries against my chest, squeezing me as though she's scared I'll let her go.

I'm never letting go.

"Shhh," I coo, stroking her hair. My cock is alive and hard as fuck as it presses against her stomach. She doesn't seem put off by it, though. She keeps her tight grip on me. "Let's get you in the car, and you can tell me what happened."

I guide her to the passenger side—because I'm gentlemanly as fuck when it comes to Bethany—and open the door. As pretty as she'd be shoved into the backseat with her dressed pushed up her hips, I help her into the front and toss her backpack onto the floorboard between her legs. When I snap her seatbelt for her, her glimmering eyes meet mine.

Adoration.

Need.

Relief.

Heat.

The look in her eyes is a flipbook of emotions—all of them revolving around her desire for me. I swipe away her mascara tearstained face and kiss her button nose before closing her in and hopping in the driver's side. The engine is loud, firing away as I gun it down the road. I should be more discreet, but I can't help it. I lose my fucking head when Bethany is in my space.

Her scent.

The sad sounds coming from her lips.

The way her mind seems to be filling up the car with unspoken words I can almost taste.

Reaching over, I give her thigh a squeeze before taking her hand. She grips it tightly, desperately, making my cock strain against my jeans. I want her hand wrapped around my dick, but this will have to suffice—for now.

"I hate my sister," she chokes out. "She's a selfish, judgmental, bratty bitch."

"Go on, Doll. Let it out." I wink at her.

Her smile is shy, but reserved just for me. "She never cares about what I want. Tonight, all I wanted was to have a perfect dinner with you."

I bring her hand to my mouth and kiss her knuckles. How can I not?

"I'll give you everything you want and more," I assure her, biting at her knuckle before soothing away the sting with my lips. This time, I rest our conjoined hands in my lap.

She chatters on about how much she hates her sister, and it makes me hate her too. If it pleased her, I'd cut the cunt's throat at Bethany's feet. She can splash in the blood puddle, dirtying up her shiny shoes, and my cock would get hard at the squeals leaving her lips.

In due time.

For now, the most pressing matter is getting Bethany home—where she belongs. Safe from prying eyes and bitchy sisters. Away from fucks like Dillon who insert themselves too fucking much into her life.

The drive is long, and after some time, she falls asleep.

Poor thing was so emotional, she exhausted herself. She'll need her rest for later.

I'm glad she sleeps for the last leg of the journey. She continues to slumber even after I shut off the car. Her eyes flutter when I open her door and pull her into my arms, but I kiss her nose, and she relaxes. It takes some shuffling, but I manage to wrench the bunker door open. When I left earlier, I made sure to leave the AC on. The space has cooled, and I worry she might be chilly in her frilly dress. As I lay her down on the bed, she finally wakes. Her stomach grumbles, and I chuckle.

"Why don't you relax and I'll make you something to eat?" I suggest.

Her brows furrow. "I made you the most delicious dinner. I'm so disappointed."

Sitting down beside her, I cradle her cheek with my palm. "I'll buy you all the ingredients you need to make it again tomorrow night. I promise. Now, sit tight."

She nods, her eyes taking on a dreamy quality—the same stare she gave me after we had phone sex. My dick lurches in my jeans, but I ignore it for now. My precious new doll is hungry. Stalking out of the room, I head into the kitchen, surprised to find the refrigerator stocked full of things Tanner knows I like. If he were here, I'd tell him my approval. I'll have to mention it later.

I'm not much of a cook, but I do manage to throw together a quick dinner—scrambled eggs, some hash browns, and a side of applesauce. I pour her a giant glass of milk that almost spills over, but stop it just in time. I hope things will stay this way and I won't ever have to starve train her.

No, this is Bethany. She won't try to run.

Run.

Run.

Run.

She wants to stay.

Mine.

Mine.

Mine.

Grabbing one of the two TV trays tucked between the shelf and cabinet, I place her dinner on top and look over the arrangement. Deciding something's missing, my eyes roam to the obnoxious vase of black roses Tanner left on the kitchen table as a welcome home gift, and I stalk over to it, yanking the biggest rose from the bunch. Pain stings my palm as the thorns cut into me, but all I can do is smile.

I'll make this good for her.

So fucking good.

Placing the rose on the tray, I carry it into our bedroom. Bethany sits primly on the bed, using a compact mirror to finish wiping away the smudged makeup. When our eyes meet, she flashes me a smile. As soon as she sees the tray I place on the bed, her grin widens.

"Oh, thank you," she squeaks, her cheeks turning pink. "This is so nice."

I sit down beside her and take her hand. A gasp escapes her when my blood smears against her palm.

"You're bleeding," she rasps. Bringing my hand to her lips, she presses kisses to the punctured flesh, and I'm mesmerized by the way her plump lips turn crimson with my blood. I want to paint her entire body with it, then fuck her until I die.

"It's fine." My voice is husky and my dick is throbbing against my jeans.

She frowns as I reluctantly pull my hand from her grip and pick up the spoon. I shovel some eggs onto it and gesture toward her with a nod of my head.

"Open up, Doll."

Her bloody lips part without argument. She's fucking perfect. Fucking mine. I feed her the eggs. Bite after bite. Then the hash browns. Our eyes never leave each other.

"I'm thirsty," she breathes, and I hold up the glass of milk. She drinks it greedily, a small rivulet escaping the corner of her mouth and hanging from her jaw. Leaning forward, I lap at her—like a cat to a bowl of warm milk. When I pull away, she hands me the half empty glass, her eyes flickering with flames of want. Setting it back down on the tray, I start spoon-feeding her the applesauce. A glob falls to the slight swell of her breasts above the top of her dress, and I toss the spoon onto the plate, sliding my hands to her ribs. The moment I lean in, her breath catches.

She's excited.

So goddamned excited.

As if I'm about to give her everything she's ever wanted in this life.

I can practically feel her thundering heartbeat dancing in cadence with my own.

Her need—her motherfucking desire for me—is irresistible.

I lick away the sweet splatter of applesauce, but the moment I taste her, I can't pull away. I suck on the flesh until a pleading whine escapes her.

"Are you still hungry?"

"N-No," she says quickly, and I pull away from her, flashing her a smoldering grin.

"Get comfortable. I'll return in a moment."

Collecting the remnants, I walk into the kitchen with purpose, deposit the tray, and grab the rope Tanner procured before heading back to my Bethany. When I enter the space, she's already kicked off her shoes and is fidgeting with the knee-highs as she stands beside the bed.

"Leave them on," I order, dropping the rope in a heap at my feet.

Her cheeks burn bright and she nods. "What now?"

I prowl over to her, admiring the way her white dress is stained with my blood on one side of her ribs. "Take your panties off."

She tears her hazel eyes from mine. So shy, my perfect doll. But she's also obedient. Her hands slip under her dress and she begins pushing the fabric down her thighs. Before she can get very far, I kneel in front of her and take over.

The moment I smell her arousal, I begin to unravel. Flashes of my Bethany from all those years ago flicker in my mind. When we'd been curious and in love. Before it was all ruined by my mother.

The Bethany standing before me is someone more beautiful. More perfect. She's not manipulative or too strong for her own good. This doll is soft, pliable, mine.

"Do you want me to take off my dress?" Her voice is a quivered whisper.

I look up, a heated smirk on my lips. "I quite like this

dress on you, Doll. When I fuck you, I want to be able to fist it in my grip."

Her cheeks blaze red and she lets out a choked sound. "This is real. This is happening."

Rising to my feet, I tower over her. She's young, so young, but I'm not a pervert. I know she's a woman despite her frilly dresses and lacy panties.

"I'm nervous," she squeaks out.

I slide my fingers into her silky dark brown hair and tilt her head back so she's staring up at me with wide hazel eyes.

"Do you want me to put on the wig?"

What?

"I brought it with me in my backpack." She gestures to the discarded bag on the floor.

"So, you know I've seen the website?" I ask, my voice hoarse with need.

Her shoulders lift in a shrug. "I thought it was a high probability."

Uncertainty flickers in her gaze. I'll have to fucking fix that.

"Never wear that wig again. Burn it," I growl before pressing my lips to hers. The moment she lets out a moan, I devour her pouty mouth. She fists my T-shirt, her breaths coming out sharp and heavy as I consume her. Slipping my hand between us, I move it under her dress and slide it to her pussy.

She practically drips with need.

Bethany wants me.

Dragging my finger along her seam, I let it linger on her clit. She lets out a needy moan, and her hips buck forward, seeking my touch. I rest my foot on the side of the bed, then draw her leg up over mine, opening her to me, exposing her beneath her dress. Then, I'm diving beneath the fabric, on a hunt for her slippery center. Her untouched pussy doesn't gape like the whores I'm used to. Even open to me, she's still as tight as ever, only confirmed when I push a finger inside her.

"Oh God," she chokes out.

"Shhh," I murmur against her lips. "I just need to feel you—all of you."

Her whimpers sing to my cock, and it pokes at her, begging for attention. I rub my thumb across her clit, enjoying the way she rocks her hips in a circular motion to chase my touch. I'm so focused on pleasuring her, I snarl when her hand touches my cock through my jeans.

I pull slightly away to glare at her, my hardened gaze meeting her curious and unsure eyes. Shy even. She's nothing like the forward whores. Bethany wants to pleasure me, but she doesn't seem to know how…or perhaps she fears I might not like it. I groan, my look smoldering her, letting her know I really fucking like it.

I want to be rough. Hurt her to claim her. Follow my instincts. Release the monster inside. But I know I have to be different with her. She's different from anyone before her.

"You're mine, Doll," I remind her, not wanting her to ever fucking forget.

"Yours," she agrees, her voice breathy. "I want it to be you. To lose my virginity to you."

"You're not losing anything," I growl, urging another finger into her tight body. "I'm taking it from you. It belongs to me."

Her pussy drenches further with arousal, my cryptic words turning her on even more. With each thrust of my fingers inside her and circle of my thumb over her clit, she begins to lose control. She clutches onto my shirt with one hand and awkwardly strokes at my cock through my jeans with the other. It's not enough. I want inside her.

"Come, Doll. I need you so fucking badly, and I can't wait forever."

She moans and tilts her head to the side, baring her pale, slender throat to me. Like a vampire seeking his dinner, I dive in, nipping the fuck out of her flesh. She cries out, and I taste metallic blood on my tongue. Instead of her crying or shrieking at me, she comes.

Holy fuck, does she come.

Her body trembles violently, her tiny pussy clamping down around my fingers in a death grip. I continue to rub her even as her orgasm subsides. Her knee, the only leg she's standing on, buckles, but I catch her. Lowering my leg, I give her a tiny push, and she falls back on the bed, staring up at me in awe.

"You bit me."

"You're a beautiful bleeder."

At this, she beams. Fucking beams at me. Goddamn, she's perfect.

Reaching behind my neck, I grab a fistful of my T-shirt and pull it over my head in one swift motion. Her gaze rakes across my tattooed flesh, and she bites her bottom lip. Since meeting Tanner, he's introduced me to the world of lifting and keeping my body fit. I've always been naturally lean and muscular, but now I'm cut from stone.

Every muscle is stronger than before. I can crush a throat with just my fist.

"This is so much better in person," she breathes.

As I watch blood trickle from the small bite I gave her, I can't help but agree. In person, I can smell her. Fucking taste her. My entire body trembles with the same sensations I feel when I want to kill someone. All consuming. Intoxicating. Out of control. Except, it isn't her life I want to destroy, it's her pussy. I want to tear her up from the inside and leave my mark on every part of her. Looking back, I feel stupid when I consider my level of dedication to Jade. I can hardly think about her these days without my own monster mocking me. I was younger and blinded then. I thought she was the best replacement for Bethany, the closest I'd ever come—but I was so fucking wrong. I should have known fate would bring my real Bethany. My perfect doll.

Now, all I can see is Bethany.

She's so perfect, all the past attempts feel like massive failures.

I pounce on her with a growl, and our teeth clash together painfully. I'm ripping at her dress, yet I don't want her to take it off. My mind battles with a thousand scenarios. There's so much I want to do to her, it's maddening me.

"Master," she breathes, her palms cupping my cheeks. "Stay with me. I want your attention on me." Her request is more of a desperate plea. She wants to be loved by me so badly, she can't stand it. My eyes bore into hers as I shove her dress up her hips.

"You're making me crazy," I admit, my words a shocked whisper.

Her smile lights up the entire goddamn room. I fumble with my belt and jeans. The moment my cock is in my grip, I glare at her.

"I can't go slow or soft or gentle. I want to fucking hurt you." My jaw clenches, and I hate my brutally honest nature.

Her hazel eyes darken. "I liked when you bit me. I'm not a porcelain doll, Master. I'm *your* doll. You can't break me." The challenge in her voice makes the tip of my cock weep with need. With a roar, I tease her opening that's slick with desire.

So many dolls I've broken. Ruined. Killed. But not this one. This one tops them all. I'm keeping her forever.

Mine.

Mine.

Mine.

"You don't know what you're asking for." My tone is deadly.

"You. Can't. Hurt. Meeeeeee!" She screams the last word as I drive myself into her tight hole in one forceful thrust. Her fingernails claw at my shoulders and tears leak from her eyes. My fingers find her jaw, and I grip her to the point I know I'll bruise her perfect skin. Her eyes clamp shut, and she trembles.

"Look at me," I breathe against her wobbling lips.

Her eyes pop open on command.

"You're beautiful, and I've never been with a woman who's felt as good as you do." Her features soften at my words. Sweet little Bethany doll. She loves her compliments. "Your pussy is wet and so goddamn tight around my throbbing dick. You saved it just for me, didn't you?

You felt me. Watching and waiting. I was always coming for you…it was just a matter of time before I found you."

"Kiss me," she begs on a hiccup. "Please."

Loosening my grip on her jaw, I slide my palm to her breast over her dress. Our mouths meet, and I can't even kiss her softly. I need to taste more of her. She whimpers when my teeth pierce her bottom lip, but she doesn't complain. Her fingers slide to my buzzed head, and she scratches her nails through it. I feel like she's had plenty of time to adjust to the size of my dick, so I thrust hard inside her as we kiss frantically.

I fuck her bare because she's mine.

I fuck her hard because she's mine.

I fuck her to the point of pain because she's mine.

Her body is tense beneath me, so I seek out her clit. I like when her body drips with need for me. When she gets slippery between her sweet pussy lips.

"Oh God," she cries out. "That feels…that feels…better," she pants.

No, Doll, it feels fucking amazing.

Soon, her body is shuddering uncontrollably and her pussy milks my dick as she fights between the pain and pleasure. I lose myself inside my Bethany. My own release comes with a roar, my seed spurting deep inside my doll. I coat her with my masculine essence and own her.

"My name is Beth," she whispers against my ear.

I lap at her bloody neck and smile. "I know."

CHAPTER FIFTEEN

~ *Neoteric* ~

Elizabeth

My entire body is on fire. Muscles screaming in protest. Flesh burning from bites and friction. My brain spinning so fast, smoke seeps from it. It's him. Master or Monster or whatever his name really is. He's intense, and I think he's obsessed with me. The thought causes my lips to quirk up.

Pulling away, he regards me with a curious stare. It's as though he's searching for something in my eyes. Hesitation, maybe? Regret? Well, he won't find those things. I'm consumed by him. I've never felt so high and wanted and revered in my entire life. Sure, I have groupies, if you will, on my fetish site, but this is different.

This, I can feel all the way down to my toes.

My heart aches and my brain bleeds.

What's churning through my veins is dangerous. To him or me, I'm not sure.

"Now that I've been inside you and tasted your lips, I'm not going to be able to stop. I won't stop." His tone is cold almost—a threat wrapped in a somber warning. I shiver.

"Nobody's asking you to stop," I tell him bravely.

His brown eyes narrow at me. "I want to take your dress off and see all of you."

I chew on my sore lip and nod. Everything feels bruised and used, but I'm already excited for him to take me again. His cum leaks out of me, and I like the way it feels. My heart thumps in my chest. We didn't use a condom. It makes me wish I wasn't on the pill. Just to have the possibility of us being bound by more than just this overwhelming connection. I shake the stupid thought from my head as soon as it manifests.

Elise is right, I'm sick.

These aren't logical thoughts.

Yet…I can't stop them from whirring in my brain. I certainly can't stop from saying them.

"I want to be with you like this always," I whisper, shame coating my voice.

He frowns, and I know I've ruined it. I'm too eager. Too obsessed. Too high off his undivided attention. Drunk on his possessiveness.

"You want to stay here?" His dark eyebrow arches, and it makes my thighs quake with need.

"I do."

I do want to stay with him. Forever. To never to feel lonely again.

We both stiffen at my word choice, but I can't help but flip through a girly fantasy that has no place in a situation where I just slept with a man I don't even know. *You do know him.*

I'm confused, yet everything feels so clear when I look at him. It's as though I'm seeing for the first time in my life.

He sits up, then slides off the bed. Up close, I realize his beautiful tattoos cover mottled scars. What caused such damage? A car accident, perhaps? I want to ask him, but decide we can chat later. Right now, I want more of him touching and tasting me.

Elise told me about sex once. She said the first time is awful and hurts. She was right about the last part, but I found no awful in the pain. It makes you feel alive. Anchors you to the moment so you can remember it, relive it over and over.

The rest of his clothes get kicked off while he devours me with his gaze. I raise my hands in the air, waiting for him to undress me. The growl in his throat is one of approval. Once the dress is gone, he drinks in my bare breasts. Dolls don't wear bras.

"You're not going anywhere," he tells me simply, his jaw clenching in an almost furious way.

I nod and eye the rope in the corner. "Are you going to tie me up?"

More heat floods to my sex. He must like that idea. His still wet, limp cock bobs back to life, and I can't believe that big thing was inside me. I'm on fire from where he took me, but crave more of the burn.

"Lie back. Close your eyes. Sing me a song," he barks.

I do as he says, singing the nursery rhyme he seems so fond of. My voice isn't the best, but I sing it extra carefully so I hit the notes and my voice doesn't crack. I want him to like the song. The heavy pounding of his bare feet signals him pacing. Lifting my lashes slightly to sneak a peek through them, my heart stammers. He's tugging at his hair, looking at the saturated mess on my inner thighs.

Reaching down, he grabs his belt before waltzing over to the bed. "Open your legs wider," he barks. "Don't stop singing."

My body trembles with trepidation. Can I handle what he is?

Thwack.

Oh God.

Ouch.

Thwack.

Pain. Hot, searing pain ignites over my exposed sex.

"I'm sorry." He almost sobs as he hits me again.

A small cry rips from my chest, and it takes all the willpower in the world not to close my legs completely and hide from him. To tell him no.

I won't, though. I can't.

The thud of him dropping to his knees and hitting himself in the head makes my soul ache. My thoughts drift to the scars hidden beneath the monster inked over his skin. Maybe he was abused and damaged. We are all damaged somewhere along the line. It's not a bad thing.

"Let your darkness flood out, Master," I choke out, encouraging him. "Soak me in it. Drown me. I can take it."

My words are like holding a flame to his fuse. My eyes squeeze together as he stills his breath. His hands seem to worship over my skin as he binds my ankles and ties them to each end of the bed. I have no idea what he's tying them to—maybe the bed frame below?—but I don't care. I love the fact that my pussy is still wet from his climax and stinging from the belt.

I didn't break. I didn't fade. I didn't tell him no.

He's keeping me. He's really keeping me.

Next, he binds my wrists, but he doesn't tie them to anything. I rest them above my head on the pillow, hoping my boobs look good on display for him. I don't dare open my eyes to look. I return to singing his song, the words dying in my throat.

His mouth is on me.

Oh. My. God.

My eyes fly open, and I stare in shock as he laps at my sex, licking away the pain with his soft yet powerful tongue. His dark eyes bore into mine, pinning me with just a glare. Owning me. Making promises I don't understand but want to. The magic he creates with his tongue is out of this world, easing the burning from moments before. Healing me. I thrash and beg, overcome with sensations I've never reached before. He makes me feel tingles up my spine and the hole he violated with his cock throbs and contracts. So easily. I don't even understand it. I don't want to understand it. All I know is I love it. I love everything about this new, mysterious man in my life.

The pain.

The pleasure.

The small flicker of light in his ever-growing darkness.

I'm still trembling from my orgasm when he climbs off the bed and disappears. Moments later, he comes back wielding a big knife.

"W-What's that for?" I whisper. I should be worried about him hacking me to pieces and eating me or something, not about how delicious he looks with an evil glint in his eyes. I shouldn't be wondering if he'll fuck me again.

"I want your blood." His brown eyes are melted

chocolate, warm and delicious.

"All of it?"

He laughs, surprisingly boyish, and my sex clenches. "No, Doll. I just want it. On you. On me. I want to own it. To own all of you. I'll make all the bad good again."

His words make me melt. "You're going to cut me?"

"I'm going to mark you so everyone knows your mine," he states, his voice possessive.

A whimper escapes me. "I want them to know I'm yours." I don't even know who *them* is, but it's true.

"Close your eyes," he murmurs as he climbs on the bed between my spread legs.

Closing them, I'm rewarded with a worshipping caress over my stomach. I'm expecting the bite of the knife, but instead, he inches his cock back inside me. He's careful and gentle, and it makes tears spring beneath my closed lids. What's wrong with me? How can I fall so hard and fast for someone who hasn't even told me his name?

Nothing, I decide. Nothing is wrong with me. I'm happy, and that's all that matters. I've been searching for happiness for as long as I can recall, and this is the first time I've felt like I've belonged in this world.

"My cock belongs in you. I'm going to fuck you all the time," he tells me, his words chopped and gritty. He's on his knees, lifting my bottom to rest on the tops of his thighs. Every part of me down there hurts and begs for mercy, but I don't want him to reward me with it. I want to hurt. To feel him. For him to leave me with the lasting pain so I know whom I belong to.

"I'm going to own all your holes. Your tight ass and perfect goddamn mouth."

I whimper and smile. "I want that. I like the way you feel stretching me to the point it hurts."

He grinds the heel of his palm against my clit, and I groan, not sure if it's pleasure or agony. "Stay still, keep your pretty eyes closed, and let me make you bleed."

The first slice is shocking, painful as hell—a small fire licking over the skin. I choke out some tears as his assault begins just to the left above my naval. The slow movements are torturous. A rivulet of blood slides down my ribs and tickles me. Tears stream down from my eyes, and I bite hard on my lip to keep from sobbing.

He's marking me.

I don't want him to stop.

I want him to make me his.

Elise would certainly think I was crazy now.

Am I?

I'm suddenly distracted from my thoughts and the pain. With his rock hard dick situated inside me and hand drawing pleasure from me, it's easy to ignore the sears of pain from getting carved across my stomach. He's careful and doing it with great care, I can tell. Not too deep and with steady movements.

"You're my doll. My everything. My Bethany," he murmurs.

I'm dizzied by his words and his assault on me. My heart lurches with disappointment at being called the wrong name. For a brief, jealous moment, it makes me wonder if he does this to other girls, or merely misunderstood when I told him my real name.

"Mine," he snarls, the word spoken so viciously, it's every bit as sharp as his blade.

His body covers mine and our skin slides against each other. My blood is slippery between us. I moan when he smears his hand across my battered stomach and goes back to massaging my clit, this time with his fingers. Everything is too intense, yet not enough. He's fucking me and he hurts me and I just need more.

"Master," I plead. "I need…"

The point of the blade digs into my throat where he bit me. It stings, but nothing like my stomach. I like the scald of it. I find myself seeking it. Leaning into it.

"No, Doll," he breathes against my mouth as he brutally bucks into me, "too much. This isn't to scar your perfect, pale flesh."

He pulls the knife away, and I whimper, but then his mouth is on me, replacing the blade, his tongue probing the slit in my flesh as he seeks my blood. I'm dizzy and lightheaded and in love. He pinches my clit, then twists it so hard, I nearly pass out from the pleasing pain. It hurts. It feels good. It's not enough.

With a screech from my lips, he buries himself so deep inside me, I don't know if he will ever not be a part of me. My body jerks beneath him, high on the endorphins zipping throughout me. This signals his own release, and he's once again coming deep inside me.I find myself wishing the door to the exit would become stuck and that I'd be trapped here with him. For him to fill me up with his cum until we suffocate from each other's love. If I don't take my pills, we'll be bound by a creation of love. I'm losing sense of reality, but I don't care. He's pulling me into the darkness, and I'm letting him. Gulping it all in—in hopes I'll drown in it.

Blackness. Beautiful dark abyss.

Waking with a start, I look around, but he's no longer in the room. White gauze is wrapped around my stomach and I'm no longer bound by my ankles or wrists. Instead, rope hangs heavy around my throat. I touch my sore neck, noticing I'm bandaged there too. The bed is a bloody mess, and it's dry and flaky. I must have been asleep for hours. The thought makes me smile. I climb out of bed and marvel over the fact that one end of the rope is tied to a leg of the bed. There seems to be plenty of slack to allow me to explore. On trembling legs, I wander out of the room and down the hall, finding him sitting at the kitchen table staring at a laptop.

"Hey," I croak out.

His dark gaze snaps to mine and he stares at me in appreciation. It sends currents of excitement coursing through me. "Hey."

"Why'd you leave?" My tone holds a hint of hurt.

Standing, he strides over to me, his delicious body bare except a pair of low-slung jeans. My mouth waters for a taste. I'm drawn into his powerful arms, and he cradles me, raining kissing down the top of my head.

"You're the most beautiful thing I've ever had the pleasure of seeing. And now I've feasted on you in more ways than I can count. It only makes me hungry for more," he growls. His palms roam to my bare bottom, and he clutches me there. "How are you feeling? You lost quite a bit of blood."

"I feel a bit woozy," I admit, defeat in my voice.

He chuckles, and it vibrates my chest. "Don't sound so upset, Bethany. I'll get you something sweet to perk you up."

He's so adorable about it, I don't even correct him. Truth is, it's close enough. I like that name. He helps me into a chair, then starts rooting around in the kitchen. I admire his butt as he moves about the space. My skin is cold and I shiver, but I like being on display for him. He eventually locates a soda and pours it into a glass. Once he's set that down in front of me, he opens a package of oatmeal cookies.

"These are my favorite," I tell him with a wide grin. "Thank you."

His brown eyes shine with an emotion I want to see more of. Adoration. Love. Desire. Want. So many flicker in his warm gaze. I want them all aimed for me, always.

"What's your name?" I ask.

His features darken, and I immediately chastise myself for ruining the moment. "In time, Doll."

I chew on my bottom lip, disappointed when he sits back down at the laptop. His attention is gone from me, and it stings. I want it back.

"I like when you call me Bethany."

His eyes dart back to mine. "I like when you wear that rope around your bloody throat like a necklace. So. Fucking. Beautiful."

I melt under his praise. "Does it make your cock hard?"

His brown eyes are liquid heat as he stares at me. "Fuck yes it does."

"Good."

When he starts to turn back to his screen, I have this overwhelming urge to distract him from it. I rise from my seat and take his hand.

"I need you to hurt me some more. I like it." I know these types of words provoke him, and that's exactly what I wish to do.

Fisting the rope, he twists it around his wrist, then yanks so hard, I nearly fall into his lap. "Hurt you where?"

"Everywhere."

"In time," he growls, his eyes soaking up every cut and bruise marred on my skin by his hand. "I like you naked, but I prefer my dolls to look pretty in their dresses."

"Dolls, as in plural?" I whisper, my brows crashing together.

"Just you, Bethany," he assures me. "There is only you."

CHAPTER SIXTEEN

~ Youthful ~

Benny

"**D**OLLS AS IN PLURAL?" SHE whines, her face crumbling.

"Just you, Bethany. There is only you."

For now. I don't tell her about my angry boy doll named Tanner just yet. I still haven't decided what to do with him.

"I got something for you."

Her eyes widen, and she bites her bottom lip, wincing when the small mark there reopens and a cherry of blood blooms. I attack like a bloodthirsty animal, desperate to suck on her. I debate bending her over the table and stuffing my cock back inside her, but my cell has been buzzing nonstop in my pocket since she sat on my lap. It's distracting and annoying me to the cusp of insanity.

"Answer your phone," she says, giggling against my lips, "but first, tell me where my gift is."

I smile and nod toward the stolen vanity. Bouncing off my lap, she hurries to look it over. Inside the drawer, she will find some panties I handmade just for her.

I take my attention from her perfect, unflawed back,

my dick hardening at the prospect of having a blank canvas to decorate. When she began singing in the bedroom hours ago, my mind stumbled into chaotic memories of the past.

The juices between her thighs screamed at me to scold and punish the dirty doll.

It was her not putting up a fight, keeping herself open for the discipline, accepting who I am, that brought me back from the edge of the old me.

My phone begins to hum again, and I yank it from my pocket, barking down the line. "What?"

"Monster," Tanner greets, his voice smooth and unfazed. "I thought after your active night you'd be in a better mood. How're the new digs working out for you? Well…I see, *Master*."

Thud.

Thud.

Thud.

I can't speak. Think. Breathe.

My eyes scan around the room, looking in every corner for the cameras that must be installed down here.

Motherfucker.

Fucking spying cunt.

Wrath like a raging entity all its own morphs and screams under my skin that feels stretched too tight over the bones beneath.

His dark chuckle penetrates my ear. "Stop looking, Monster. The cameras are everywhere and for your own security."

For his watchful fucking eyes, more like.

"Your new doll is quite exquisite," he praises. "I

enjoyed watching you with her. It amuses me that you like for her to call my name when you're inside her. Oh, Master—"

I throw the cell at the wall, startling Bethany when it explodes and falls to the floor like jagged glass rain.

"Who was it?" she whisper-yells in my direction, holding her hand to her chest.

Rushing toward her, I cover her body with mine. "Doesn't matter. Get dressed." I point at her torn, ratty dress, my chest heaving with rage. "Now."

"Why?"

"We're leaving. I'm taking you home. I have things to do."

"But I don't want to…" Tears well in her wide hazel eyes.

I hold my hand up to stop her mid-flow. "You need to know what I tell you isn't to be debated. I'm your master, and you will do as you're told."

She nods her compliance, but the tears brimming her lashes leak free.

"I'll come back for you," I promise, my voice softening. This doll needs the extra assurance. "I just need to sort some things first, okay?"

"Okay."

The car ride back to drop Bethany off at home is quiet. All my plans are going to have to change. This intrusion can't be tolerated. I won't be kept like a pet for his games and pleasure. Not fucking happening.

It's four a.m. by the time I reach her house. The lights

are off, a blanket of darkness shrouding the house.

"Do you want to come inside?" Her voice is meek and soft.

"I can't, Doll."

She fumbles with her fingers, lowering her eyes to her lap. "Did I do something bad?"

A sigh pushes past my lips. "No," I placate, hitching my hand under her arm and pulling her across the seat into my lap. She curls up against me like a bunny rabbit and hums in contentment. Closing my eyes, I just hold her.

Heat suffocates me, and panic seizes my chest as I jolt awake. Sunlight bleeds in through the windows, blinding me. Sweat coats every inch of my body, dripping like I've been dipped fully clothed in a bath. The air is thick and smoggy like a sauna, and I'm gasping as I try to breathe it in. As soon as I take stock in my surroundings, I realize where I am. In my damn car. My heart rate spikes. Goddammit. We fell asleep in full view. Anyone could have seen us. So fucking stupid. Bethany stirs in my lap and lazily opens her eyes.

Lowering all the windows, I blast the AC and check the time.

Nine-thirty.

Fuck. Fuck. Fuck.

My mind whirls at how careless I was. If anyone saw us and called the cops... I can't even finish that though without wanting to go crazy as shit.

"You need to go now," I tell her, peeling her sweaty body from mine.

Her eyes scan the area and a yawn passes her lips.

"Okay. Thank you for my new gift. That vanity is beautiful. I'll bring your other gifts with me next time to set them on top." She's unsure of her words, testing me to see if I intend to take her back there again.

"The doll?"

She searches my face in confusion. "All of them," she states with hesitation.

What the hell is she talking about all of them? I just gave her the one. It was one I found online—one I sold in the past.

"I gave you one. A very special handcrafted one with silky brown hair like yours." I know this because I made it. "The wig was hand sewn with donated human hair." Well, not exactly truth, but dead people don't need their hair anymore, so I like to think of it as a donation. "You got more dolls?"

Her eyebrows scrunch together and her bottom lip protrudes out. "The rest aren't from you?"

She's irritating my already frayed patience. "Doll, what the fuck are you talking about? What do you mean the rest?"

She shifts in her seat before answering. "Someone has been leaving me gifts. I thought they all must have been from you."

"How do you not know who is giving them to you?" My tone is hard, accusing.

"Because they just show up at the house." Just like the doll I gifted her.

Motherfucker. If this shit is Tanner playing more games, I'm going to lose all control with him. He is taunting me into killing him.

"I do have some guy on my fetish site that is always on and commenting," she says. "Maybe it's him."

"You don't *do* that shit anymore," I tell her, my tone severe. "You're *my* doll. My eyes only." I wait for any attitude, but there is none. Just a nod in compliance. "Do you remember the user's name?"

Her hands dive into her backpack and she pulls out her phone. With quick moving thumbs, she brings up the site, then hands the phone to me. She's enlarged the screen, hovering over the user.

Dollkeeper

A few yards away, the front door to her house opens. Fucking Kami steps out and jogs toward a bright pink mini Cooper.

"That's Elise's best friend," she whispers, dropping low in her seat.

Oh, I know who she is.

Her stupid girly car pulls away, and I mentally chastise myself for losing the opportunity to get some good old payback.

All will come in due time.

"Should I be worried about the person sending me things? He knows where I live. He's been in my room."

My attention is brought back to my precious little doll and I cup her cheek. "I'll deal with him."

She doesn't ask what that will entail, and it makes me want her more.

"Go get some rest. I'll be back for you later."

When I arrive at The Vault, Tanner is already prepared for

me. I find him sitting in the office assigned to me with his hands up in surrender.

"Lick those wounds, Monster. I'm not dealing with you puffing your chest out over something as small as me having surveillance installed. You need to move into the twenty-first century," he spouts his guarded crap at me, showing me his playing hand.

So explanatory. So defensive. So pathetic.

He rattled the monster's cage and shit himself when the chain broke on its leash.

I smile at him, keeping my hand close to my chest. Confuse the poor bastard.

"Glad you enjoyed the show." I shrug, moving toward him and pushing his feet from their propped position on my desk to the floor.

His cool façade slips, and there's a wary shimmer in his eyes. He stands, and I take the seat he's kept warm for me. He's been sitting in here waiting for quite some time.

Power. I have it—not him.

He throws something at me, and I catch it before it can hit me in the face.

My tolerance of his games and need for dominance over me is waning. *Not long*, I tell myself.

"What is it?" I demand.

He grins and shrugs his shoulders. The once relaxed, put together character he always wore like a second skin around me is slipping more and more.

"Where's the fun in that? Open it. Enjoy. I have an appointment coming in soon, so I'll be on my way." With that, he waltzes off, closing the door as he does.

His appointments are job interviews. For some

reason, he likes to be the first stopping post of anyone who comes through the doors of his club. Discretion is a key component any employee must possess when working for Tanner. His club has stayed below the radar of the law thus far for a reason. He's particular about who he allows to work for him, and the generous paycheck reflects why his employees are so loyal. His methods ultimately keep his clientele happy in the knowledge that their identities and fetishes are kept zipped tight behind handpicked lips from the owner himself.

I've watched Tanner in action. He has a way of unnerving even the best of us—unraveling our binds and stripping back the layers one at a time.

Sometimes, the interviewee doesn't even make it to the chair before he strikes them out as a no.

He likes power, and rules his empire as a true leader should, but he made one mistake.

Me.

No one owns me. I'm the master of my own story, *and* the master of his. He just doesn't know it yet.

He will.

Soon.

Ripping the large envelope he tossed at me, I tip it up and a cell phone falls free.

Replacement for mine? He works fast.

Picking it up, I study the small device. There's nothing on it but a video stored in the memory.

More games, Tanner?

Clicking play, my gut clenches.

It's a shower room of some sort and a naked old fuck is being kicked to shit by what looks like a few different sets of legs.

"Lift him to the camera," someone orders, and shuffling sounds out before the broken, beaten face of the man I once called Papa takes up the entire screen.

"Drop him," the voice demands again, and he falls to the floor with a thwack. The camera pans out, and the torso of one of the men comes down behind him, grabbing a fistful of his hair and pulling his head back.

"Spread him open for me," someone else growls, then shoves his dick into my father's mouth while the other guy holding him forces himself into his ass.

They assault him as he bucks and gargles. I don't know why the fuck I would need to see this or what the purpose of it is. I hover my finger over the end button when the one with his cock shoved down my daddy dearest's throat pulls out and begins stabbing him repeatedly in the neck with what looks like a screwdriver.

He was mine to kill. Why the fuck would Tanner do this? Why now, without even consulting me first?

For power.

A show of his reign over me, my inner monster warns, roaring at me.

I already have his punishment for spying on my doll planned, but the intense need to scream in his face ricochets inside me, hitting every nerve ending.

Arghhh.

I throw the cell across the room, and it explodes into a thousand pieces against the wall, much like my own when I got his call last night.

Rounding my desk, I'm out the door and hightailing it down the corridor. I ignore Lucy standing outside

Tanner's interview office and push straight in. I also ignore the brunette he has sitting in front of his desk. His eyes flare wild at me from across the room as I stalk toward his desk.

"Not a good time, Monster," he growls, standing up and coming chest to chest with me. We're both breathing hard like two dragons waiting to take flight and burn everything below us to cinders.

"What the hell was that?" I demand with a snarl.

"Not the time, Monster." His eyes bore into mine, trying to convey whatever the fuck it is he's thinking.

Well, guess what, asshole, I'm not a mind reader.

"I'm not your fucking Monster," I bellow, the rage forming my words. "I want to know what the hell you were thinking," I add, expecting the visitor sitting frigid in the chair to run for the exit so she doesn't get caught up in the inferno about to engulf the room.

"What *I* was thinking?" He laughs, devoid of humor. Leaning down, he fishes something from a briefcase sitting under the desk.

He slaps an envelope at my chest—the one I'd posted days before to my father to boast about my new doll.

Motherfucker.

I should have known Tanner would have eyes there. He has them everywhere.

"I did what had to be done to prevent your truth from being revealed. You think…" He stops talking mid-thought and turns to look at the nobody girl still sitting across from us. "Get out," he orders, and she jumps to her feet, scurrying to the door.

Turning back to me, he pokes at my chest with his

finger. "You think he would have just sat on that information? He wouldn't call anyone like fucking Dillon Scott? Do you know it was those girls they used against him to get him talking? He loved them, he wouldn't let you keep her."

My head swims with this information. I wasn't thinking straight when I sent the letter. But he went behind my back to kill him without asking me. A power move he took to keep me in line. To remind me who the king of this dark underworld he brought me into and kept me safe within is.

Am I truly free?

Safe?

My own monster?

If someone is always pulling the strings, then no.

A heavy fist pounds against the door, piquing Tanner's interest. "What?" he grounds out past clenched teeth. I've shaken the beast. Good.

Lucy hurries inside, her long, wavy blonde hair hanging loose in front of the large tits spilling out the top of her red leather tank top. "Kami's back."

Relief loosens his jaw and he nods a confirmation before she turns on her heel and leaves, but not before giving me a wary eye glare.

"I have Luke following up on the woman you just nearly spilled your identity in front of. You may need to clean that up," he snaps.

"There was nothing said she could or would decipher as anything."

He's fucking paranoid. No one knows I'm alive. I doubt some random woman is going to have even heard of the doll killings, let alone think I could be him. He is over-the-top, and I don't have time to chase some idiot just because he tells me they're a threat. In reality, he just hates that she saw two beasts come head-to-head and he wasn't the victor. He shows weakness when he's with me.

"I'm going to spend some time with Kami, and I'm not to be disturbed," he bites out, leaving me in his wake.

Yeah…well, fuck you.

Fuck Kami.

Fuck you both.

"I've had enough. I want to hide away with you forever. Why can't we just go?" she questions, her voice a slight whine on the other end of the line.

She is going to have to learn her place with me. This pouty lip crap only works when she's in front of me and I can bite the offending lip.

"People will look for you," I explain with a grunt. "They won't accept you just up and left without reason. You have people looking out for you, like that detective. He would find you or try anyway."

She's silent for a few minutes before her wispy voice groans down the line. "You're right. Elise would be like a dog with a bone driving everyone crazy."

She doesn't question the fact of how I know she has a detective friend, which pleases me. She's already learning the dynamics of Dolly and her Master. I will be taking her away from it all, but the less she knows to accidentally tell her sister, the better.

"Get some rest, little doll," I tell her, my tone dark and

promising. "You're going to need all your energy for later."

I end the call and throw the newest cell phone down on the desk. I made Lucy take it from one of the bar boys. My fingers tap at the laptop Tanner left open when he made his dramatic exit. He will be too caught up in Kami right now to even think about it.

I want to see what her insides look like.

Her blood decorating my hands and my favorite knife.

There's a locked file for all his cameras, but one is open already, so the password isn't needed. I click on the small image, and it expands to fit the full screen—the cells he had made for me to take my dolls to. I click the arrows, and more camera angles come into view. They're everywhere. He was going to watch my doll in my bed and in the cell. Some things are sacred. Just for me.

Going into the operations, I delete all but one camera view, then rename it to match another file he has on there. I smile. *I was broken from a young age, Tanner.* I can't be tamed or picked up and molded by anyone else's hand. The monster already killed its master years ago. It can never be leashed by another.

Leaving his office, I go through to the bar. "Whisky neat," I tell the guy serving.

A warm body brushes up against me, and I turn to tell whoever it is to fuck off, but a grim looking Lucy greets me, her full pink lips pressed into a firm line. "Cassian is on the war path." Her blue eyes narrow. "He's looking for you."

"He's done with his little pet already?" I seethe, tossing back the entire glass placed in front of me.

The amber liquid reminds me of the man now looking for me. Let him look. Let him come to me.

"I thought *you* were his pet," she retorts, disgust lacing her words.

Moving too quickly for her to reach for the knife she's always fiddling with, my hand closes around her slim throat as I back her up against a pillar. "What did you say?"

She doesn't fight the hold. Her eyes are ablaze as she chokes out. "K-Kami had to leave. Elise called her crying over the state of her sister."

I release her, and she gasps, rubbing at where my hands just were. "What do you mean the state of her sister?"

"Apparently her new boyfriend roughed her up, but she's not talking."

Elise, ever the drama queen.

And she just did me a favor without even knowing it.

"Benjamin," Tanner bellows, gaining more than just my attention. Careless of him.

I leave the bar without another word to Lucy and follow Tanner back down to his office. He slams his laptop closed, and hairs spring up over my body, making me hyperaware. Nervous energy tap dances over my ribcage as I wait to see if he's noticed the fuckery I just implemented with his computer. Anger radiates off him like he's radioactive and about to blow.

"Luke called," he finally speaks, and I relax. He hasn't seen it.

"And?"

Luke is the lackey who gets the shit jobs of following people and checking up on them. The kid's also really fucking good at hacking into computers.

"That woman I was interviewing when you came in and had your hissy fit."

I let his insult join the collection of shit Tanner's done to piss me off and will pay for later.

"Spit it out," I growl.

"Don't," he warns, raising a finger at me. "This is serious. She was picked up from town by a Marcus James, Dillon Scott's partner."

My wiseass demeanor diminishes.

Fuck.

Motherfucker.

Shit. Fuck.

"A cop? So, she's one of them?"

His jaw ticks. "It would appear so. Luke's running her file now, but this doesn't bode well."

I crack my neck and glare at him. "There's no way she would recognize me or even have me on her radar. Dillon *killed* me. He has no reason to think otherwise."

"You better hope that's true," he bites out. "I'm waiting for my informant at the precinct to call me with any information. She will need to be dealt with, Benjamin."

Yeah, doesn't everyone. There is no doubt that this is the reason she was sent here in the first place. Probably by Dillon "Sniff Out a Criminal" Scott. Tanner eliminates anyone who is a threat to him—even a minor one. Despite it just making him look guiltier of hiding shit, he'll *deal* with her immediately.

"I have a meeting to collect the second shipment of Law's purchase. I want her dealt with before I get back. I'll forward any information you'll need. Do you need another cell phone?" He scowls at me.

"No, Lucy got me sorted with one. Get the number from her." And with that, I hightail it out of there.

I have work to do.

Fun to have.

Revenge to inflict.

Dolls to punish.

CHAPTER SEVENTEEN

~ Fresh ~

Dillon

Jade's been suffering from false labor, something called Braxton Hicks or some shit. All I know is I haven't slept a wink worrying about her and my unborn child. Leaving her this morning after she accused me of being overbearing was the last thing I wanted to do, and the text from my mom telling me she's arrived at the house for the day brings a smile to my lips. Jade wouldn't dare accuse my mom of being overbearing, so guess who called in reinforcements as soon as I left the house?

I walk into the precinct, and my stomach plummets when Marcus comes barreling toward me, a tense glare boring into me. His normally slicked back dark hair that makes him look like one of those celebrity dicks on television hangs down into his eyes. He's not put together whatsoever. Panic flickers in his grey eyes.

"I haven't even had coffee," I warn him.

"Josey did something stupid—and without permission." He sends a scathing look over his shoulder at a cowering Josey, who is hiding behind a cup—a cup of fucking coffee, I bet.

Walking past him and straight toward her, I take the cup from her hand and point toward the door. "Go home."

She blanches, then rolls her eyes. "You haven't even heard what I did yet."

"I don't need to. This will still be my reaction once I've heard."

"Fine," she huffs. "But I did well, and you can thank me when you realize it." She swipes up a jacket on her way past Marcus's desk and pushes through the double doors to the exit.

"I'm sorry. I had no idea she would do anything without the okay," he sighs, running a hand through his dark hair. At least now I know how it got messed up in the first place.

"You look like shit," I tell him, swigging the beverage I confiscated. It's bitter and hits the spot perfectly.

His scruffy jaw clenches, and he flashes me a pained look. "Lisa is still ignoring my calls and she hasn't been back to her place in days." The motherfucker looks heartbroken, and I feel bad for the guy.

"What about her job?" I suggest. "Just stop by there."

"She's in school," he admits, his cheeks turning ruddy with embarrassment. "I thought I told you that."

"You told me she was twenty-five," I grumble.

"Oh, she is," he says quickly in defense. "She did some traveling, so she started her degree late."

I'm bored already. "So, what did Josey do?" I ask now that I'm caffeinated.

"She went to The Vault." He flinches.

Christ.

"She said a guy called Tanner interviewed her and

had an argument with some guy he called Monster right in front of her."

Who the fuck's Tanner?

"Anyway, she said she took some discreet pictures so we can see if our Cassian Harris is her Tanner guy.

Who calls someone Monster?

"Scott," Graham from tech yells from his office, doing a come here wiggle with his hand.

Why are tech guys so fucking weird? Too clever for their own good must be hard on their social skills.

"Get the pictures," I bark to Marcus, who gets straight on the phone, telling Josey to email the images over.

"What you got for me?" I ask Graham, taking a seat on the end of his desk.

"The IP address you wanted me to trace?"

"Yeah." I nod, wanting him to continue. I needed to put my wife's mind at rest and track down the pervert obsessed with little Beth.

"It traces to a computer used there." He taps his finger over his computer screen.

No fucking way.

I check to make sure I'm seeing it right.

The Vault.

Christ!

My cell vibrates, and I pull it from my pocket. Elise's name flashes across the screen. "Hey, kiddo."

"Dillon, can you meet me somewhere not at the house? I'm so worried about Beth, and my friend Kami who was supposed to come over, but she hasn't. I don't know what to do," Elise rattles out quickly. "I don't want to worry Mom when she has so much going on with work and—"

"Elise, calm down," I interrupt. "I'll meet you at Rosa's Coffee House on the corner of Main and Third."

She lets out a relieved sigh. "Okay. Thank you."

"Twenty minutes?"

"See you then. Bye."

Damn, these women in my life are going to have me in an early grave at this rate.

"Marcus, let's go."

"You want to tell me where we're going?" my partner asks, rubbing a hand over his eyes. He's tense as a motherfucker. This dude needs to get his love life in order. Stat.

"I need to pop in and see Elise, then we're going to see Mr. Harris at The Vault."

His head perks up and he shifts in his seat. "You got something?"

I pull my cell from my pocket and hand it to him. "Look at the first image in the picture section."

Taking the phone, he fiddles around. "Cute, but I don't get it." He flips the screen around, showing me MJ wearing Jade's heels and dragging her giant handbag. Frowning, I snatch the phone. Once I park in front of the coffee shop, I swipe the screen, handing it back to him with the username and some of the comments Dollkeeper made on one of Beth's images.

"The user is from The Vault," I tell him. "How fucked up is that? All roads lead to this Harris guy. There has to be a reason for that."

I get out and walk the few yards toward the coffee

shop, stopping when I notice Marcus is still in the car staring at my phone.

Fucking hell. If he's getting off to little Beth's picture, I'm going to punch him in the junk.

The car door opens just as Elise comes out of the coffee shop carrying two to-go cups. She sees me and grins.

"Is this a joke?" Marcus shouts, holding up the cell phone.

The coffees in Elise's hands drop to the concrete and hot fucking liquid sprays up my leg, making me holler in shock.

My eyes drag from the mess on the ground up to Elise, who is holding her hands over her mouth. I follow her gaze to a stunned looking Marcus.

"What's going on?" I ask warily.

"Shouldn't that be my question?" Marcus asks, incredulous, fury causing his voice to shake. "What the fuck is this? And how do you know Lisa?" He's still holding out my cell phone and talking to me, but staring at Elise.

I'm so fucking confused, I feel like I just fell into the twilight zone and no motherfucker is making sense.

"I'm so s-sorry, M-Marcus," Elise stutters, tears welling in her hazel eyes.

I look between the two of them.

"Marcus, this is Elise, as in Elise and Elizabeth, Stanton's twin girls." I want to shake him to get him to start making sense.

His mouth drops open, then closed. His face screwing up in pain, he doubles over, then stands back up and turns, cussing.

"Someone better start talking," I growl.

"I lied to you. When I saw you and you didn't recognize me…I was hurt, but then excited. I've had a crush on you since I was ten years old," she stumbles out, waving her hands animatedly.

"How could you not recognize her?" I ask, stupefied.

His hands go to his hips as he looks over at her with mist in his eyes. Shaking his head, he looks at me. "The twins were around thirteen when I last saw them, and when I say I saw them, I mean briefly, in passing at the precinct." His eyes widen, as if he just realized something. "Oh God. How old are you, really? Oh God, Lisa."

Lisa?

No fucking way. Marcus and Elise. He could be her father if he had her when he was young. High school maybe, but still. Fuck, how could he not know?

"I'm nineteen. Legal. I wouldn't do that to you," she assures him, and I feel sick at the unwelcomed image of Marcus and little Elise flashing in my mind. Jade is going to lose her shit over this. She loves Marcus and was so happy he was finally moving on. I haven't had the heart to tell her there was trouble in paradise.

"I can't fucking deal with this. This is bullshit," he snaps, his grey eyes turning hard with fury. "You're so far out of line here, I don't even have words for you right now."

A sob escapes her throat.

"I'll be in the car," he growls at me before slamming the door shut.

Perfect.

A barista peeks her head out the door and stares at Elise's fracturing figure. "I'll clean this up. Do you want them replaced?"

"No thank you, sweetheart," I call out as I usher Elise away from the mess and walk her down the sidewalk away from Marcus's glaring eyes. "I don't even know where to begin with this, Elise."

"I'm sorry. I broke it off because he wanted me to meet you and I knew it had gone too far," she hiccups, making a snorting sound.

"Too far would have been at the start when you told him petty lies to deceive him." I pinch the bridge of my nose in frustration.

"You're mad at me too?"

Fucking girls. When MJ is a teenager, she's not allowed out of my sight. This shit is too much. Girls are devious little shits.

"I'm not happy," I grunt. "Go home, Elise. I will stop by after work and we can talk then. All of us."

She nods, and I give her a hug and a quick kiss to the top of the head before leaving her to sort herself out. Opening the car door, I collapse into the seat and stay silent for a few minutes. Marcus passes my cell back to me, shaking his head.

"How can I be so fucking stupid? So blind?"

I shrug and let out a sigh. "This is new territory for me, man. I don't know what she was thinking, and I don't really know how I feel about it, only that it's fucking weird."

He swallows and shoots me a pained stare. "I feel like a pervert. She's just a kid. Twenty-five was an issue, but I thought she was worth it, you know? And now…fuck," he snarls as he pounds his fists into the dashboard. "I'm twenty years older than her for fuck's sake."

"Once the shock has passed, you can replay things

and think rationally. She played you, Marcus. You're not to blame."

His jaw tightens as he looks out the window, dismissing anything else I have to say on the matter.

We arrive at The Vault and Marcus is still not himself. I picked him up a little while ago after a three-hour lunch break for him to get his head straight, which gave me a chance to check on Jade and MJ and actually have lunch with them for once. I wanted to tell Marcus to take the rest of the day off, but I need his cool head for when we go inside. Cassian Harris gets under my skin and makes me want to throttle him until all that snarky attitude falls right out his fucking ass.

"Can you just wait here?" a young woman asks. Her face is tense and bright red. She's flustered and out of her depth. "Where is Lucy?" she hisses to another employee, who shrugs his shoulders

"I don't know. She's not back in until later," he tells her.

She looks up to the ceiling, then pulls a radio from a clip on her hip. "What room is it he said?" she asks down the line.

Marcus huffs and darts his eyes from her to the guy moving past us with a drink tray. "Hey, man, you seen Monster around?" Marcus asks, and from his tone and hesitation, I know he feels like an idiot for using the name Monster.

The boy looks to the door behind me, then to Marcus. "I don't think he's back yet. I'm sorry, who are you?"

"No one," I answer for him. "Run along, kid."

The boy looks me over, then back to Marcus before exhaling and disappearing down the corridor.

I flick my eyes to the girl pacing the floor a few feet away talking animatedly on the radio. Trying the handle on the door behind me, I grin to Marcus when it gives under my hand. Inching it open, I slip inside and take in the simple décor, mediocre desk. No personal pictures. My eyes drop to a shattered cell phone on the floor. I reach down and pocket the sim card before Marcus is standing in the doorway, summoning me to get out.

I don't make it past the threshold before the woman is standing there, narrowing her eyes on me. "That's not the right office," she bites.

"My bad." I smirk.

"Yeah, right."

She leads us farther down the corridor to another room—a different office from the one we first spoke to Cassian in, laid out pretty much the same, only a much bigger space.

"Gentlemen, what can I do for you?" he asks, standing from his chair and gesturing for us to take a seat. Once we're seated, he lowers himself back into his own chair.

His focus is torn between us and a laptop in front of him. I'm just about to open my mouth when his body goes rigid. His hands shaking, he pulls the screen closer to his face and jolts upright, running past us like a Tasmanian devil.

"What was that all about?" Marcus asks the question running though my head.

Getting up, I round the desk, looking at the screen

to see what spooked him. A woman lies naked and covered in blood inside what looks like a glass cell. I take off after him, searching. A ruckus draws me to his location. He roars from inside another room and comes crashing through the door. I catch a glimpse of an empty glass box through the sliver of space growing smaller as the door closes.

"What the hell is that on your computer?" I growl as he barrels past me. Grabbing him by the lapels of his jacket, I stop him before he can pass me. His body is solid in my grip. He's heavy, and not easy to manipulate into moving where I want him.

"Release me right now, before you regret ever breathing my air," he seethes, the look covering his features morphing him. He doesn't even look human.

"You're not leaving until I get answers," I warn him.

"Then arrest me, Detective, or get your hands off me."

I release him, and he jerks his shoulders before pulling at the bottom of his suit jacket to straighten it. He's out of sight before I can follow.

"D," Marcus says, and it's grim as fuck.

"What?"

"Josey's house. There's been a break in and she's not there. There are signs of a struggle," he tells me, the color in his face fading to white.

"Check the images she emailed over," I snap, racing to get out this fucking place.

On the way to the car, I'm already fiddling with my cell phone, popping out my sim card and inserting the one I retrieved from the office, hoping it will have something substantial enough to get Cassian down to the station.

I need to grill him. To break him. To find out why his name keeps popping up along with his damn club all over the place lately.

"It's empty," I growl, shutting the car door. I open the texts. Nothing. Contacts. Empty. Images. One video.

I click over it and nearly spew my guts.

How the fuck has this not been reported to us?

Grabbing Marcus's cell from his hand, I dial the number for the prison and get put through to four different departments before finally reaching the right one. Pass the fucking buck much, assholes?

"I want the status of an inmate. Steve Stanton. Immediately."

The woman on the line makes a sound of frustration. "I'm sorry, Detective Scott. Stanton is no longer a prisoner here. The details have been faxed over to your department."

I end the call and want to throw the fucking thing. The email screen comes up from when Marcus was looking through his emails and the images stare up at me from their tiny focus. Acid burns through my veins.

No.

No.

Impossible.

No.

Enlarging the image, I can faintly hear Marcus in the background saying my name.

The fucking world tips on its axis.

No.

No.

No.

I'm dreaming. I'm stuck in a fucking nightmare that resurfaces over and over again.

Brown eyes—eyes I'd never forget.

Benny.

He's different, but the same. A new buzz cut. Scruffy beard on his face. Tattoos.

No.

No.

No.

Monster. The video of Stanton on a phone from his office. All the connections back to The Vault.

Monster is fucking Benny.

How?

"Call Elise. Tell her to get Beth out of the house and to go to the station," I order, my words sounding distant to my own ears.

"What the fuck is happening?" he bellows.

"It's him. It's Benny," I stutter, dropping the phone and turning the car on. "I need to get to Jade."

He's already on the phone barking out orders. "Elise, get your sister and meet me at the station." He curses. "No, goddammit, do it now." A pause. "What do you mean? Well, text her to meet you."

He looks over at me, the fear, confusion, and alarm written all over his face matching my own. "Elise isn't at home. She's going to call Beth."

Fuck.

I snatch up his cell and dial her number. It just rings. I type out a quick text.

Me: Your new boyfriend is Benny. He's your fucking brother and dangerous. Get out of the house now.

I'm sending a unit to meet you.

"Call some uniforms out to Elizabeth's house," I urge Marcus as I barrel along to my house. I mount the curb before throwing it into park and race from the car up the driveway, bursting through our front door that isn't locked.

Jade thinks it's safe.

That she'll always be safe.

We killed him.

But…we didn't.

Fuck.

"Dillon," Jade screeches, scolding me for bursting in and scaring her. I pick MJ up as she toddles toward me and grab for Jade, pulling her against my chest.

She comes willingly, sensing my need—my urgency to feel her, smell her.

"You're scaring me, baby. What is it?" she breathes against me. I don't want to tell her. Ruin her. Break her. But I can't lie to her. Her world is about to crumble around her, and I'm not sure I'll be able to find her and bring her back from the rumble.

"Dillon," she urges, her voice cracking.

Fuck. I'm so sorry, baby.

"It's Benny."

CHAPTER EIGHTEEN

~ *Untried* ~

Benny aka Benjamin aka Monster

I SEND THE LINK TO Tanner and smile over at a now-bloodied Kami. The feed will tell him she's in his office, but she's not. She's here in the bunker he built for me and filled with fucking spy cameras. The bitch was easy to take. She may be a fighter, but she's small, and I've had plenty of practice with the feisty ones.

My dirty doll liked to push my buttons and fight back.

My mind wanders back to when Kami realized what was happening and who had her. Her motherfucking worst nightmare.

"Let me out of here. Now," she screams, *pounding her fist against the clear wall.*

"No," I taunt her.

"Cassian won't let this go. I'm his."

I snort in response. "Well, he is mine, and he was naughty."

She kicks and screams for a bit, and I relish her fury. Her strength wanes with her outburst, and the look in her eye when she accepts threatening words about her Cassian aren't going to keep her safe from me...

I prepare myself as I unlock the cell door and step inside. She rushes me, arms poised for a boxing match. Shame she's no match for me. I land a brutal blow straight to the side of her head, knocking her skinny ass out. Her body slumps to the floor like meat being prepared for a butcher's knife.

Stripping her of all her clothes, I take in her body littered with scars, both fresh and old. Bruises in a variety of colors make her skin look like a patchwork quilt. She whimpers, her eyes fluttering open. Confusion furrows her brows before remembrance makes her pupils expand in warning.

Her foot rears out to kick at me.

Nice try, bitch.

I grab her foot and twist until I hear a snap of bones. Her scream is otherworldly as she howls in pain. The dumb bitch tries to scramble away from me, but she's a fucking gimp now. With a mangled ankle, she drags the useless part of her behind her as she crawls. Her motions are slow and filled with pain. I'm going to make it so she can never run away. Seizing her other foot, I twist it too, the crunching and popping beneath her flesh making my heart race with glee. She sobs so hard, vomit spews across the inside of her cell. With two broken ankles, she'll no longer be able to kick. And if she keeps acting like a vicious whore, I'll break her wrists too.

Seeing the rage and hate in my eyes, she cowers away from me. This bitch was brave as shit when her precious Tanner was following her around like a lost puppy. She's no match for me or my fury.

These two assholes fucked with me.

Now, I'm going to fuck with them.

"Wh-What are you g-going to do?" she demands through her tears, her fight still brimming just below the surface. I want all fight within her destroyed. I'll rip it from her piece-by-piece.

"You think I'm going to rape you, dirty skank? Rape your used ass?" I ask in astonishment.

Her gaze darkens. "Fuck you."

I snag her by the throat and squeeze. She claws at me, but three hard whacks against the cell wall has her falling limp in my grip. I release her throat and stare at her useless body. Blood from the back of her head smears the Plexiglas. Yanking my knife from my belt, I drag it along the inside of her thigh until she rouses. The cut isn't deep, but it's enough to draw blood and remind her of the severity of her situation.

Her eyes are wide as she attempts to retreat from me. There's nowhere to go, Dumb Doll. I smear my left palm along her bloody thigh, and she curses at me before going fucking wild once again. I spin her in my grip and pin her to the floor face down.

"You've lost," I snarl against the shell of her ear as she wiggles.

"He'll kill you," she chokes out. "Fuck you!"

At this, I laugh and shove my knee between her thighs. She screams and writhes. With my hand on the blade of my knife near the base, I tease her cunt with the hilt.

"What's that, Dumb Doll? You want me to fuck you?"

The bitch is feisty like my pretty little doll once was. Puts up one hell of a fight, but it all leaves her the moment

I push the handle of the knife into her dirty hole. A strangled sound pours from her, saturating my soul with satisfaction.

"This is what defeat feels like," I breathe against her hair as I brutally fuck her with the handle. The blade digs into my palm, no doubt slicing open my hand, but I relish in the pain. Her body goes limp once more.

Dumb Doll passed straight the fuck out.

Not such a badass now.

With a grunt of irritation, I yank the knife from her pussy and stare down at her. The blood from her thigh is everywhere, and now oozes from her used cunt. I smirk, knowing it will drive Tanner fucking mad wondering if I put my cock inside her.

My cock is for Bethany, but he doesn't need to know that.

Reaching forward, I run my finger along her thigh through her blood. When I flick my tongue out and lick the metallic liquid, I frown. She doesn't taste delicious as fuck like my pretty new doll. Bethany is sweet, but sinful. Decadent. Perfect.

This dumb bitch tastes like all the rest.

Knowing Tanner will have figured out the camera switch by now and be heading this way, I close Dumb Doll's cell and head back outside to collect my other doll waiting for me in the trunk. I can't wait to see the look on Tanner's face when he sees his precious girl in the new cells he created and the surprise once he realizes he will have to live beside her. Angry Doll will be positively furious. I laugh out loud, imagining his face red with rage.

After drugging Kami and dumping her in the trunk

earlier, I went for the cop girl. She was easy to take. Too easy for a cop. I dumped her in with Kami, but she was still out cold by the time I arrived at my bunker, which made it easier getting the feisty bitch down here without having to worry about the woman cop too.

Cop Doll stirs as I open the trunk, but not enough to cause problems. Scooping her up, I bring her down to the cell on the right, leaving the middle one empty. I lay her on the floor and debate carving her up for fun, but it's more of a "fuck you" if she's alive when *he* arrives.

I check my watch and roll my shoulders. Tanner will be here soon. I can feel it. This is it. The moment to show them who the real power player is here.

I get in position just outside the door to the cell room behind one of the racks lined with canned goods and lie in wait. Quickly, I send out a message to my doll, telling her we will be leaving tonight and to be ready. She doesn't reply straight away, and I hope it's because she's asleep and will be well-rested and primed for more of my love making. I thought I was going to have to improvise with her, but she's not like the others. She doesn't need to be locked away. She's loyal. Perfect. Mine. And she can stay out of her cell all the time if she stays that way.

My heart begins to race when I hear the opening of the latch followed by footfalls and calls for Kami. He really fucking loves that bitch. I hope he likes looking at her now that I've had my way with her. Serves him right. He crossed a line.

You like games?
You like watching?
He doesn't notice me hiding in his frantic search

for her and comes to a stop at the cells. His fist smashes against the one with his Kami splayed out on the floor, but he's no match for the thick glass.

"Kami." His voice breaks, and pride washes over me like warm sunshine. He tries to open the door with his key, but struggles. Asshole should have known the first thing I would do was swap out the locks. Moving up behind him, I shove at his back. He's so distracted with his misery, he falls, off-guard, and stumbles into the open middle cell. Realization hits him with the sound of the door clanking shut and the lock snapping into place, my face staring at him through the opaque wall.

"You can watch your precious Kami all you want now." I smirk.

He smashes his closed fist against the joining wall, but, again, he's powerless against it. "Don't do this, Benjamin. I gave you everything." He breathes heavily, closing his eyes.

"But it wasn't free, was it? It was all a game to you, and it comes at a cost."

He clenches his jaw. "Why hurt Kami? Did you—"

"Rape her?" A smile curls my lips up. "She was the price. Your debt. You thought you could play with my doll and I'd allow it? You know me better than that," I sneer.

"I helped you with her!" he bellows, his mask of control slipping away.

"By spying on me? By fucking interfering? What about the gifts and notes? The disgusting comments on her page? Did you think I wouldn't know it was you?" I scream. "I had your own man, Luke, trace the IP address." Marching over, I retrieve the iPad from the table and smack it up against the cell. "It traced back to the club. To you!"

His face contorts, then all the lines thin out, and the cold, icy stare he gives me causes my insides to solidify. "That's not mine, Monster."

CHAPTER NINETEEN

~ *Now* ~

Elizabeth

"Mom's coming home early from her trip," Elise seethes, hot tears spilling down her red cheeks.

I won't be here.

I'll be with *him*.

When I spoke to him on the phone earlier, he promised I wouldn't have to wait long.

"Good for her," I snap.

This makes my sister cry even more. "Y-You've fallen off the deep end, Beth. First it was the website, then all the dressing as a doll in public, and now? Now, you've got some sadistic boyfriend who abuses you. You need help."

"Are you pregnant or something?" I hiss out in fury. "All you ever do is fucking cry these days."

Her hazel eyes widen in horror. Call it twin intuition, but I have a feeling I may have hit the nail on the head. Just like she somehow figured out my boyfriend is a sadist. Absently, I finger the bandage at my throat that won't stop seeping blood through the gauze. When Mom gets home, I may have to have her stitch it up for me.

"You've turned cruel," she sobs.

I gape at her. "Me? You've always been cruel. Maybe I finally grew a backbone and wanted to stop living in your stupid shadow."

She winces, as if I've struck her. If she keeps this shit up, I *will* strike her. I can't watch her cry any longer. Storming up to my room, I start throwing stuff into my pink rolling suitcase. Now that I know the other dolls didn't come from Master, I don't want them. I pack the beautiful one with the silky brown hair into the luggage, but abandon the rest. Also, I toss in my notebook, my many handmade dresses, and my makeup. What I don't pack are my birth control pills. I don't want them anymore. Elise's sobs penetrate the air around me, and I stop to listen. It sounds like she's talking to someone on the phone. Probably tattling to Dillon about me. My phone buzzes, and I groan. I expect Dillon, but find a message from Jade.

Jade: I thought maybe just you and I could go to lunch one day before the baby comes. Girl talk. Dillon kind of gets into dad mode and I know that can get annoying. I'd love to see you and treat you to someplace special.

I love Jade. I truly do. But I see straight through this. They're coming at me from all ends. An intervention of sorts. I'm not interested.

Me: Sure. Sounds fun.

I'd rather lie than tell her I'm not coming back. Ever. Soon, Master will be here for me, and we're going to be together in his bunker away from the judgmental world. We'll make love and I'll be all his. Forever. Eventually, I hear the front door slam and Elise's engine fires up in the driveway. As soon as she's gone, I let out a sigh of relief.

I drag my suitcase downstairs and set it near the door, wanting to be ready to leave the moment he pulls into the drive.

I'm startled when the doorbell rings, but half a second later, a grin tugs at my lips as I smooth out my dress and prepare to see him. When I open the door, I'm saddened he's not here yet.

"Elizabeth Stanton?" a pretty blonde woman asks.

"That's me." I frown at her in confusion. "Do I know you?"

Her blue eyes brighten and she beams. "I'm a friend of Monster's. He's a little tied up with some friends and asked me to fetch you for him. Are you ready?" She motions at my suitcase in the doorway.

Apprehension floods through me. "Um…yeah. He didn't tell me anyone would come for me." I pull my phone out to text him, but she stops me with a laugh.

"You know men. They can't plan for shit. Don't worry," she whispers, her blue eyes flickering with amusement. "I know all about your secrets, Pretty New Doll. And your secrets are safe with me."

"Oh," I murmur.

When she reaches for me, I flinch, and she simply chuckles. "Let me take a look at this, precious. Looks nasty." I still as she peels away the bandage on my neck. Her eyes darken, and she licks her voluptuous lips in a hungry manner. "This cut needs tending to." She digs her finger into the hole, and I cry out. "It's deep."

My hands shake as I take a step away from her. Hot blood runs down the side of my neck, dripping into my cleavage. As soon as my phone starts buzzing, I read the message, hoping it's Master telling me he's on his way. What I see confuses me. I gape in shock.

Dillon: Your new boyfriend is Benny. He's your fucking brother and dangerous. Get out of the house now. I'm sending a unit to meet you.

Benny?

Benny died. He burned in the…

My mind races faster than the stampede my heart is doing in my chest.

The scars beneath the monster tattoo?

They're not from a car accident.

They're burns. The monster hides burn scars.

Oh my God.

My brother.

Master is Benny?

I blink several times in shock, waiting for the disgust to come. The anger. The hurt. But I don't feel any of that.

I've slept with my brother? It should make me feel wrong…right?

Tears sting my eyes, yet the longing in my heart doesn't subside. Everything has become too messy and confusing in the blink of an eye. If Master—er…Benny, were here, he'd tell me to calm down. He'd promise to take care of it all. Make everything make sense. His mouth would press against mine, and he'd consume me like before. It would be natural and beautiful.

Soulmates.

I suppose, deep down, if I'm truly honest with myself, this doesn't surprise me. It should, but as soon as I learned he existed, I felt a change inside me. An emergence. My soul comprehending the brother I never knew was so much more than just that. I recognized the eyes. I understood his obsession with me had been something deeper than I could comprehend. All the signs pointed that way. But they told me he died. Maybe I needed to tell myself that, or maybe he did die, in a sense. And like me, he was reawakened.

He's alive.

And he's my Master. He's mine and I'm his.

We're meant to be together.

My heart soars.

"Let's go, precious," the woman says, her voice hard. "Time's running out."

My phone buzzes again.

Master: We will be leaving tonight. Be ready.

The way her eyes dart to my cell and jaw flexes has dread pooling in the pit of my belly. My eyes lift to the pretty blonde before me who now fiddles with a knife that looks too sharp. Why would she need that? When Master—er…Benny, had the knife, I wasn't afraid. I trusted him. But this chick? I have the urge to run. Now.

"Don't think about it," she snaps, the sweet bubbly façade gone. "Get in the car or I'll cut a hole the size of Texas in the middle of your chest and drag your beating heart into my greedy little hand."

I swallow down my fear as tears roll out. He didn't send her. "W-Who are you?"

She flashes me a pretty smile—too pretty to be some psycho threatening to cut my heart out. "You can call me Dollkeeper." My pulse skitters at her words. She's the stalker. The commenter. The flash of blonde in the trees when I looked out my window. The person who brought all the other dolls and was inside my bedroom. Oh my God…the woman from the bookstore who knocked coffee all over me. "My friends call me Lucy."

Before I can process what's happening, my phone gets swatted out of my hand, clattering to the porch floor, and Lucy drags me by my hair to her waiting vehicle.

Oh God.

Oh God.

Benny, come save your dolly before it's too late…

To be continued in…
Pretty Broken Dolls
Coming soon!

ACKNOWLEDGMENTS FROM
Ker Dukey

A huge thank you to you! The reader. Benny and his dolls captured your intrigue, and you refused to let him rest. Without your persistent pestering for more Benny, this awesome story would just rattle around in our heads biting and barking at us.

Sometimes you have to itch the scratch and hope you don't break the skin.

Co-writing with Webster is always easy and fun, although she's extremely horny 99% of the time she doesn't ever mind me dousing her in a little cold water from time to time and she reels in my camp side (when I get all glitter and unicorns.)

As always my family sacrifices a lot for me to spend time writing and I can't thank them enough for allowing me to do what I love and taking a backseat when the voices are calling.

These books don't happen on their own, so a BIG thank you to Monica @wordnerdediting for coming on this journey with us and breathing the story like it is her own.

Big thank you to Webster's team for setting up the cover reveal and early reading.

The cover created by Webster is perfect as always.

Stacey over @champagneformats who always make both K's and my titles beautiful and fitting us in whenever we push our luck and surprise her with releases.

Thank you to all the incredible blogs who share the love for our titles, without you, we would struggle to get our titles out there in the hands of eager readers.

Thank you to everyone who makes time to leave a review, I can't express enough how important reviews are so thank you.

Big shout out to my wonderful group Dukey's darKER souls, thank you for all your love and support.

Special mention to, Nicky Price who keeps the ship running.

And Terrie my PA who keeps me running.

You are all wonderful. I love you.

ACKNOWLEDGEMENTS FROM K Webster

A huge thank you to Ker Dukey for wanting to write another book with me. I feel like by book three, you and I had this in the bag. We had a blast and cackled like the two witches we are whenever we'd deliver mayhem and madness. Thank you for being such a freak like me. Also, thank you for letting me take out the flamboyant parades you kept wanting to sneak into the manuscript. And thanks, *I guess*, for whipping me whenever I'd let my freak flag fly way too high and way too frequently. I'm sure glad we balance each other out. But our love for Benny will always outweigh everything. I look forward to more projects with you so we can terrorize all the people with bright shiny wicked grins on our faces. Love ya, girl!

Thank you to my husband, Matt. You're always there to love and support me. I can't thank you enough. I'll always be your favorite doll.

I want to send out a GIANT thanks to all the supportive dollies out there. Your morbid curiosity, thirst for more, or general love for villains is what has made this series such a success. Benny loves *all* his little dolls. Continue to be good little dolls and we might give you more of your beloved Benjamin. Love you guys for being so awesome and excited about our characters! (Fun fact: The title headers in *Pretty New Doll* are synonyms of the word "new.")

A huge thanks to Elizabeth Clinton and Ella Stewart and Misty Walker. Thank you always being so supportive and quick to read my stuff no matter what. You are great friends!

I want to thank the people who either beta read this book or proofed it early. You all gave me great feedback and the support I needed to carry on. You all give me helpful ideas to make my stories better and give me incredible encouragement. I appreciate all of your comments and suggestions.

A big thank you to my author friends who have given me your friendship and your support. You have no idea how much that means to me.

Thank you to all of my blogger friends both big and small that go above and beyond to always share my stuff. You all rock! #AllBlogsMatter

I'm especially thankful for my Krazy for K Webster's Books reader group. You ladies are wonderful with your support and friendship. Each and every single one of you is amazingly supportive and caring. I love that we can all be weird page sniffers together.

A huge thanks to Monica with Word Nerd Editing for taking care of another one of our precious dolly books and making it as perfect as it could be!

Thank you Stacey Blake for making this book

GORGEOUS like always! Love you!

A big thanks to my PR gal, Nicole Blanchard. You are fabulous at what you do and keep me on track! Also a big thanks to the ladies over at The Hype PR!

Lastly but certainly not least of all, thank you to all of the wonderful readers out there that are willing to hear my stories and enjoy my characters like I do. It means the world to me!

ABOUT THE AUTHOR
Ker Dukey

My books all tend to be darker romance, edge of you seat, angst filled reads. My advice to my readers when starting one of my titles…prepare for the unexpected.

I have always had a passion for storytelling, whether it be through lyrics or bed time stories with my sisters growing up.

My mum would always have a book in her hand when I was young and passed on her love for reading, inspiring me to venture into writing my own. I tend to have a darker edge to my writing. Not all love stories are made from light; some are created in darkness but are just as powerful and worth telling.

When I'm not lost in the world of characters I love spending time with my family. I'm a mum and that comes first in my life but when I do get down time I love attending music concerts or reading events with my younger sister.

News Letter sign up
www.Authorkerdukey.com
www.facebook.com/KerDukeyauthor

Contact me here
Ker: Kerryduke34@gmail.com
Ker's PA : terriesin@gmail.com

ABOUT THE AUTHOR

K Webster

K Webster is the author of dozens of romance books in many different genres including taboo romance, dark romance, contemporary romance, historical romance, paranormal romance, romantic suspense, and erotic romance. When not spending time with her husband of many, many years and two adorable children, she's active on social media connecting with her readers.

Her other passions besides writing include reading and graphic design. K can always be found in front of her computer chasing her next idea and taking action. She looks forward to the day when she will see one of her titles on the big screen.

Join K Webster's newsletter to receive a couple of updates a month on new releases and exclusive content. To join, all you need to do is go here http://authorkwebster.us10.list-manage.com/subscribfe?u=36473e274a1bf9597b508ea72&id=96366bb08e).

Facebook: www.facebook.com/authorkwebster
Blog: authorkwebster.wordpress.com/
Twitter:twitter.com/KristiWebster
Email: kristi@authorkwebster.com
Goodreads:
www.goodreads.com/user/show/10439773-k-webster
Instagram: instagram.com/kristiwebster

KER'S BOOKS

Titles by Ker include:

Empathy series
Empathy
Desolate
Vacant
Deadly

The Deception series
FaCade
Cadence
Beneath Innocence - Novella

The Broken Series
The Broken
The Broken Parts Of Us
The Broken Tethers That Bind Us – Novella
The Broken Forever - Novella

The Men By Numbers Series
Ten
Six

Drawn to you series
Drawn to you
Lines Drawn

Standalone novels:

My soul Keeper
Lost
I see you
The Beats In Rift

The Pretty Little Dolls series:
Pretty Stolen Dolls
Pretty Lost Dolls
Pretty New Doll

Titles coming soon:
Devil.
Add to Goodreads. à Here ß
Lost Boy
Add to Goodreads à Hereß

K'S BOOKS

The Breaking the Rules Series:
Broken
Wrong
Scarred
Mistake
Crushed

The Vegas Aces Series:
Rock Country
Rock Heart
Rock Bottom

The Becoming Her Series:
Becoming Lady Thomas
Becoming Countess Dumont
Becoming Mrs. Benedict

2 Lovers Series:
Text 2 Lovers
Hate 2 Lovers

Pretty Stolen Dolls Series:
Pretty Stolen Dolls
Pretty Lost Dolls
Pretty New Doll

Taboo Treats:
Bad Bad Bad
Preach

Alpha & Omega Duet:
Alpha & Omega
Omega & Love

War & Peace Series:
This is War, Baby
This is Love, Baby
This Isn't Over, Baby
This Isn't You, Baby
This is Me, Baby
This Isn't Fair, Baby
This is the End, Baby

Standalone Novels:
Apartment 2B
Love and Law
Moth to a Flame
Erased
The Road Back to Us
Surviving Harley
Give Me Yesterday
Running Free
Dirty Ugly Toy
Zeke's Eden
Sweet Jayne
Untimely You
Mad Sea
Whispers and the Roars
Schooled by a Senior
B-Sides and Rarities
Notice
Blue Hill Blood by Elizabeth Gray

Made in the USA
Columbia, SC
27 October 2017